SONGSNATCHER

BOOKS BY DEAN F. WILSON

THE CHILDREN OF TELM

The Call of Agon
The Road to Rebirth
The Chains of War

THE GREAT IRON WAR

Hopebreaker
Lifemaker
Skyshaker
Landquaker
Worldwaker
Hometaker

THE COILHUNTER CHRONICLES

Coilhunter
Rustkiller
Dustrunner
Lostlander
Sixshooter
Deadwalker
Songsnatcher

HIBERNIAN HOLLOWS

Hibernian Blood
Hibernian Charm

A COILHUNTER CHRONICLES NOVEL

SONGSNATCHER

DEAN F. WILSON

Cover illustration by Duy Phan

First Edition 2022

ISBN 978-1-909356-33-7

Published by Dioscuri Press
Dublin, Ireland

www.dioscuripress.com
enquiries@dioscuripress.com

Welcome to the Wild North

CONTENTS

Chapter

Welcome to the land of stolen childhoods.

In the grim region known as the Wild North, someone is snatching children from their cradles, using an ancient tribal music to lure the innocent away.

In a world where children are seen as the spawn of demons, many are turning a blind eye to this heinous crime.

But not Nox. Not the Coilhunter. Nox has his own kind of music. When the twang of guitar strings doesn't do it, there's always the percussion of gunfire.

ONE TOO MANY SHERIFFS

It was a few months after the collapse of the Iron Empire and the end of the so-called Great Iron War. That should've only affected the war-torn territories down south, but it didn't. It affected the Wild North as well.

You see, some folk said that now that the Iron Empire was gone, the Wild North would grow to take its old territories. It wouldn't just be the Wild North. It'd be the Wild Everything. The Wild Everywhere. Oh, you'd need more than one sheriff for that.

But right now, one sheriff was enough. That was Nox. That was the Coilhunter. He'd made a living hunting down conmen and criminals, who'd flocked to the Wild North to escape the heavy-handed "law and order" of the Iron Empire. Nox was there to give a little of his own.

The Bounty Booth was quiet that day. Logan Hardwell still wore his Iron Empire uniform, more out of habit than anything. He wasn't the worst of them, and didn't have the worst of their habits, that was for sure. He was just their attempt to keep the Wild North in its place, within its own boundaries. They paid in coils, the old currency that still had sway there. Those new-fangled *dollars* circulating down south just didn't cut it with the Northfolk. They wanted to live free. It was just funny they did it with the currency of a faction that'd been hell-bent on suppressing freedom. Folk said a lot of things in the Wild North, but no one ever said it all made sense.

"You'd think you'd be retired by now," Johnny Grin told Hardwell, making sure the Coilhunter heard as well. You see, he didn't just mean it for the bounty operator. He was one of the new up-and-coming bounty hunters who'd circled in after the Iron Empire fell, like carrion birds for the kill. Some of them were old Resistance fighters. Hell, some of them were from the Iron Empire too. So-called real-life "demons," or so the Resistance had painted them. All of them were there for the money. For the coils.

And for the Coilhunter's job.

"My old employer has ceased operating," Hardwell said, brushing a grain of sand from his shoulder.

"That's puttin' it mildly," Johnny Grin replied, smiling that cheeky smile of his, raising that one eyebrow that always seemed to move alone. He was the kind of gunslinger who gave you a bit of charm as he gunned you down. The ladies liked him. Hell, some of the men did too. Despite what the desert did to you, it didn't seem to dry out those golden-brown bangs of his. But then he was young. The desert wasn't done drying.

"But my employment hasn't," Hardwell continued, stressing the words a little to show his annoyance at being interrupted. "The Wild North is still, well, wild. The interim government has deemed it appropriate to continue payment for … your services."

Hardwell looked to the Coilhunter for that last part. Nox was by the door, leaning against the frame. That wooden building was falling in on itself, just like the Wild North as a whole. You see, Nox might've leaned, but it leaned right back. It was like the few good things that survived the desert. It leaned against the sand, against the wind. It leaned against the lawlessness. Of course, it had Nox to support it there.

And now Johnny Grin.

Johnny wasn't the first new bounty hunter to waltz on through that creaking door, and he sure as hell wouldn't be the last. You see, the criminals went up north to make their fortune, away from the eyes and arms of the law. And some enterprising lawmakers went on up after them, looking for a little fortune of their own. Of course, sometimes the law part got lost in the hunt. That was the difference between them and Nox. To him, the coils were gravy. The law was the meat.

Chapter Two

THOSE RED PASTURES

When Nox shifted at that door, and you heard him, and you saw him, you knew he wanted you to hear and wanted you to see. You knew he could've gunned you down before you glanced his way. You knew he could've made you see shadows and phantoms, and maybe stars, and maybe dirt, and then maybe nothing at all.

So, when Nox thudded on into that room, Johnny Grin turned to watch him. The Coilhunter brushed past him, acting almost like he wasn't there. Right now it seemed like all he cared about was shoving that handful of Wanted posters down on the counter, and then shovelling those mounds of coils into his coffers. You couldn't help but notice that Johnny Grin eyed them greedily. Well, he might've been boisterous, but he wasn't foolish enough to try and grab them.

"A big haul?" Johnny Grin asked. He peered over Nox's shoulder to see the monowheel outside, with an easy half a dozen bodies piled in the bounty box at the back. *Easy* might've been the wrong word, but the Coilhunter made it look that way. And the desert made it easy for you to be body number seven. Hell, it'd let you bring your friends too.

"A normal day," Nox croaked. If it wasn't the heat that dried up his throat, it was the sand that gnawed away at it. You couldn't quite reach your hand down to scratch that itch. The fall of the Iron Empire hadn't upset the Dew Distributors' monopoly on the water supplies, but it'd caused enough uncertainty that folk were hoarding theirs. It made you want to save some of your own, even when your gullet told you to gulp it all down right then and there.

Nox headed over to the bounty wall and ran his gloved finger over some of the names. Tony Two-timer, wanted for robbing the bank he was hired to protect. Gabby Hatchet, wanted for hacking off the hands of her unfaithful husband. Benjamin Boxer, wanted for smuggling in young girls in crates for the Black Silk Collective. And Sam Silver, wanted for selling counterfeit pregnancy kits, which he'd claimed could tell you whether you'd give birth to "demon" spawn, or even if you were a demon yourself. Made quite a killing on it too. Funny, that. So would Nox.

"Sam Silver, huh?" Johnny Grin said as Nox pulled down the poster. "He's small fry, that. A li'l old goldfish in a pond. Would've thought he'd be too small a catch for you, Coilhunter." He laughed. "But then maybe your high time past bein' put out to pasture. You see, me, I'm outta catch me a shark."

"Good," Nox replied. "I was gonna suggest you go swimmin' with some."

Johnny Grin smirked. "At least your wit's not all dried up."

"And neither is my gun arm. You might think the likes of Sam Silver too beneath ya, but that's how they operate. That's how they do their bad, right under the glare of the sun, right while you're glarin' at someone else. The law is the law. You ain't too big for it, and you ain't too small either."

"Whatever you say, Nox, whatever you say. Alls I know is your piece o' paper there says a hundred rocks." He prodded a dirty finger at the coil reward listed on Nox's Wanted poster. "And mine here says a lucky five hundred. Now, I don't know 'bout you, but who between us is gonna build a bigger mountain?"

Nox shuffled up to Johnny Grin, casting the shadow of his cowboy hat on the man's face. He let out a puff of black smoke from that mask of his, the one he needed to breathe with, the one he needed to nurse away the pain. "You oughta be careful where you walk, boy, 'cause you're already on my mountain."

Johnny Grin backed out of the Coilhunter's shadow and gave a nod of his own cowboy hat, and don't forget that grin. "That's the thing about dunes in the desert. What you built out there yesterday will be gone tomorrow. Well, Nox. Welcome to tomorrow."

Chapter Three

POWDER BASIN

The Coilhunter climbed inside the large outer wheel of his vehicle and kicked away the stand. He revved hard and felt the rumble of the engine beneath his seat. The giant steel treads on the wheel kicked up dust in the direction of Johnny Grin, who rode a three-wheel motorcycle known as a hyper-hog. Normally those were only used by the biker gangs, but you never could tell in the Wild North. It often had a way of surprising you.

Nox drove off, carving a path through the sand. He was on the hunt, which meant there was a sense of urgency. Sam Silver wasn't a big fish. Johnny Grin was right about that. So, that meant he didn't quite have to die today. But why waste time? Besides, the trail was only warm for so long. The bodies too.

The land whisked by around him, the curved dunes and the cracked flatlands. Sometimes you yearned for some crumb of outcropping, for some sign of civilisation, or even just a hint of life. And then other times, when you met that life, the low life of crime and nature's dark equivalents, you craved the featureless expanse instead.

Nox knew where to look first. Sam Silver was

greedier than he was careful. That meant he kept pushing his luck, kept making more deals. Some folk said you were born with your allotment of luck all dealt out. Some folk said as soon as that hourglass of life started filling up, that smaller hourglass of luck filled up too. Some folk said you were lucky if you got more than a few grains. And some folk said that that wheeling and dealing Sam Silver was bound to make a bad deal.

Good, Nox thought to himself. *Now I can bring ya in.*

You see, the Coilhunter only brought in the bad. Not the hard-up and the questionable. Sam Silver did a lot of work in the so-called grey area. Hell, he considered the Wild North as a whole to be one big old grey area. But it wasn't. It was red. Half of that was the hue of nature, and, well, you could guess what the other half was.

Nox travelled that powder basin towards one of the saloons Sam Silver frequented—and Sam didn't go there for a drink. *Good*, Nox thought again, because he wouldn't either.

Chapter Four

THE ARMOURED INN

Nox pulled on up and parked the monowheel, kicking out the support stand and letting the heavy wheel tilt onto it and dig a little into the sand. It was good that those treads were wide and thick or he'd never get around. You adapted to the desert or you died. And sometimes you did both. Told you you only got a few grains.

Well, there it was. That building looked more like a turtle shell than a saloon. The many steel sheets were riveted together, giving it the texture of industry that seemed so natural in that land. Turrets pointed out of gun slits aiming in all directions. If you had enough arms, you'd do the same.

It was a veritable fortress, which was maybe a little overkill for a rum-hole. But then again, in the Wild North, overkill was a way of life. Sometimes the only way to live at all. If you didn't empty your barrel, they would. It didn't matter who "they" were. They could be the rival gangs or the jealous onlookers, the bounty hunters or the vigilantes, the nightstalkers or the day scorpions. Hell, they could just be the grains of sand themselves.

Four heavily-armed guards stood at the entrance

to the inn.

"Coilhunter," the guards said in unison. "This ain't your jurisdiction."

"The law ain't got no boundaries," Nox replied.

"Well, we're law-abidin' folk at the Armoured Inn."

"I don't know what you're abidin', but I ain't here for trouble."

"Well, you don't look like you're here for a drink. And you don't need to be here for trouble. You *are* trouble."

"Then call me Trouble then, if you wanna make that one of my names. Just you move aside and let Trouble in."

The guards eyed each other, communicating that recurring question the criminals of the Wild North had: *Who was better to get on the wrong side of? Your boss or the Man with a Thousand Names.* A hatch opened on the side of the monowheel, and out of a little ramp half-rolled and half-waddled a mechanical toy duck. They eyed it with widening eyes until it halted between Nox's legs.

"Oh," Nox said. "I forgot somethin', didn't I? You can call us Team Trouble."

The guards said nothing, but moved out of the way, watching that toy duck carefully, while it watched them back even more careful. Nox was known for his colourful companions, and the bad folk of the world feared them as much as they feared his guns.

Nox marched on through those bat-wing doors, and the clatter they made, along with his signature heavy bootfalls, made the room grow suddenly quiet.

The card players tried a game of steady hands, and boy were some losing. The beer guzzlers tried some careful sips instead, and boy were they thirsty. The barman stopped mid-popping the cork on a bottle of dusty red. It almost felt like if he let that cork go bang, that'd start something. It'd be the first shot fired. The first blood poured. It wouldn't have been the first time a gunfight started over someone's frayed nerves. And there were a lot of frayed nerves there. After all, Trouble had arrived.

Nox let them sit and simmer for a moment, let them be uncomfortable. Uncomfortable enough to want him to leave, uncomfortable enough to want to talk. It was one thing to know where you were going and what you wanted. It was something else to know when to act and when to wait. Sometimes the silence scared you more than the gunshots did.

When finally the Coilhunter shifted, even the hardiest in there flinched. A cigar-puffing ruffian let his old stogie slip from his lips and burn a hole in the cards on the table. Like a bullet hole. Oh, there was nothing to stop his lip trembling now. The folk there watched the Coilhunter from the corner of their eyes, not willing to draw his own dark, merciless eyes their way. It was the barman those eyes fixed upon. It was the barman the Masked Menace approached.

"You," Nox barked at the bar dog behind the bar. "Dozen-gun Dan, is it?" He glanced at the side of the barman's face to see a metal plate with wires, which Dan was known for. And they said you couldn't teach an old dog new tricks.

The man was now pressing the corkscrew back

21

into the cork, fighting the pressure in the bottle. Everyone there tried to fight the pressure in the room. You see, they were trapped in a bottle themselves.

"It is," Dozen-gun Dan admitted, a little hesitantly, like admitting a crime. He nodded overhead to where a plaque bore his name. That was a bold move around those parts. Sometimes you had to enquire "Who's askin'?" before you ever dared to tell your name. Well, they knew who was asking, and they knew him by a thousand names.

Nox eyed the bottle and read the label, noting one of those titles he'd been given. "Sandsweeper Red. Year 16 since the Harvest. That's this year. That's a good year." He watched the barman fight the bottle even more, as if this year had turned suddenly very bad. "Here," Nox said. "Let me help you there." He moved like lightning. Before anyone could as much as blink, he flexed his right wrist, which loaded a pistol up his sleeve and sprang the handle right into his hand. He blasted that cork right out of the bottle. The liquor sprayed and foamed all over the counter.

"Let me help ya a second time," Nox rasped. He reached over the bar, grabbed the barman's apron while it was still on him, and yanked him close enough that Nox could wipe down the spill, making sure to show the barman that blood-red splotch that now hugged his torso.

"There," Nox said, before using that same lightning speed to slap down on the now clean counter the Wanted poster that was just begging to be seen. He unfurled it to reveal the face of Sam Silver. "Now, let me help you one last time." He prodded his gloved finger at the poster. "This man, Silver. Ya seen 'im?"

Dozen-gun Dan shook his head nervously. "Haven't seen hide nor hair of 'im," he said, trying to sound a little more convincing.

"Is that so?" Nox croaked. "Only, it looks like ya did. It looks like you knew who exactly I was lookin' for when I came through those doors there. So, tell me, Dan, are you confusin' that shake for a nod?"

Dozen-gun Dan was about to speak, but the Coilhunter raised a hand and silenced him.

"If you're about to lie again—and if I were a bettin' man, I'd say you were—let me save ya the trouble. Because you *are* in a lotta trouble, aren't ya, Dan?"

Nox reversed the Wanted poster with a clatter, revealing his sketch of the Armoured Inn, with its three back rooms, one of them marked as "demon detector manufactory."

Dozen-gun Dan glanced at the paper, then back at Nox, and he did it a few more times that Nox knew what'd happen next—what always happened when you cornered the saloon-stalker rats. They'd run if they could, like Sam Silver ran. Or they'd fight.

The bar itself shuddered, and the panels shifted to reveal a row of a dozen automated guns, all linked to the chip in Dan's dozen-triggered head. All of them pointed at Nox.

Fight it was then.

Chapter Five

DOZEN-GUN DAN

Nox dived in front of the bar before the guns blasted. The other patrons hid behind their tables, while one or two were gunned down as they tried to run for the door. You didn't run from Dozen-gun Dan—not unless you had a dozen legs to do the running.

Nox knew he couldn't stand up without being torn down. He couldn't leap over the counter or make for the door. At least one of those shooters'd get him. That was the thing about bullets. The first ninety-nine could miss you, and you'd call yourself lucky. But it only took one. They'd call you anything you wanted then—as they carved it into your tombstone. But they sure as hell wouldn't call you Lucky.

The automated guns fired in alternating patterns, saving their rounds, but when new targets emerged, the patterns changed. It made them hard to predict, and hard to counter. Nox knew Dozen-gun Dan must've had a partner in this. Few folk had that kind of technology. The Coilhunter was one of them.

He checked his belt, thumbing the capsules and orbs he'd brought with him. He went through so many, and restocked so often, that sometimes he lost count of what was there. And that was a risky thing to do in the Wild North. It was like losing count of the other guy's bullets. You kept those numbers in your skull or you'd keep the bullets there instead.

He rolled a butterfly canister between his fingers, toying with the idea of throwing it up over the counter. They were just toys themselves one time, little mechanical creatures designed to make the children laugh. And then, when he became the Coilhunter, he changed them into something else, something more—little mechanical monsters to make the criminals cry. He wasn't sure if the canister would survive long enough to discharge its contents, or if those little butterflies would last long enough to get to their target. Some of them would go for the guns, sure enough. They sensed movement, and boy did those guns move. But he only needed one butterfly to get to Dozen-gun Dan and spray its noxious fumes into his face. That'd knock him out cold. Nox could then use his gun to knock him out colder.

But he hesitated. There were half a dozen butterflies in that little orb, but there were twice as many guns to take them out. He rolled another canister into his hand. He had just the two of them, but that'd still only be an even match. And there was nothing even about sending butterflies against guns. He needed an advantage. He needed a distraction.

"You're awful quiet down there, Coilhunter," Dozen-gun Dan shouted out. "Cat got yer tongue? Or is it these here pistols? You've got two good gun-arms, I'll give ya that. But you ain't a match for my twelve."

Good, Nox thought. *Keep talkin'*. That was the thing about many of the Wild North's criminals. They just couldn't help themselves. They just had to get in that final word. It wasn't enough to gun you down. They had to gloat over your body too. But there was a problem with talking. It meant you weren't thinking. It meant you weren't watching.

"I know you're there," Dozen-gun Dan continued. "You've been houndin' us for months. Gettin' in the way o' business. Good, old honest business too. Weren't many that got hurt. Thought we'd let loose o' ya. Oh, but you gotta keep tightenin' that noose o' yours. Gotta keep houndin' the little ones, pushin' us to the brink. It's then we fight back, Coilhunter! It's then we give ya your money's worth. A dozen guns for your damn coils!"

It was then, just as he finished that sentence, that something large rolled out from the counter into the middle of the room. The guns all pointed at it, and they went into a firing frenzy when it sprang up and open, forming into the shape of the Coilhunter himself. Simultaneously two smaller orbs appeared in the air. Some of the guns turned to blast them, but both of them cracked open in time to unleash their mechanical payload.

The butterflies, made of all shapes and colours, fluttered towards anything that moved nearby. Just as Nox predicted, many of them went for the guns. One of them even went for the scarecrow version of the Coilhunter in the middle of the room, thanks to the flailing fabric, sent spinning from the gunfire. Nox stayed still on his end of the bar, but he knew Dozen-gun Dan wouldn't be still on the other. He ought to have been, if he was smart, but the Coilhunter knew one thing for sure when he faced those criminals: behind the bluster and behind the bragging, when they met him and his toys, they always trembled.

One lone butterfly zig-zagged through the gunfire and headed right for Dozen-gun Dan's face. The man scurried away on his back and elbows, until he struck the wall of bottles behind him. One bottle of moonshine shook and dangled on the edge. If he'd have been lucky, it would've fallen and smashed on the ground, diverting the motion-tracking toy to the shards. And boy did that bottle teeter. But it didn't topple. Dozen-gun Dan, eyes wide with terror, shifted a little again, drawing that mechanical insect his way. He swatted at it, but that just reeled it in. When it got to Dan's face, and he screamed, it latched on with its tiny claws and sprayed a thick green gas into his eyes. That was when he finally sat still back there, and when those dozen guns stopped shooting.

See, just like those ninety-nine bullets, it didn't matter how many butterflies missed. It only mattered the one that got through, the one that got you. You see, those gravestone makers, who worked so hard and worked so often, never got to carve the name Lucky at all.

Chapter Six

BACKALLEY WHISPERS

Nox left the Armoured Inn behind him, but not before rummaging through its back rooms and walking out with documents detailing the illegal trade routes used by Dozen-gun Dan and his criminal associates—not least of all that sneaky trickster Sam Silver. It wasn't too surprising that many of those routes led to the Burg, that central plateau-city ruled by the Dust Barons. It was surprising, however, that Silver got to trade there unnoticed. The Barons must've gotten sloppy since the fall of the Iron Empire. And that was a risky thing, that. You see, some said the Iron Empire got sloppy too.

Nox drove out to the Burg, eyeing that stunted city from the distance. The sandstone buildings almost merged into the plateau it was built upon, and if you were far enough away you'd think it just another of the desert's features. The houses and inns were all flat-roofed, and mostly level with each other, making a kind of plateau of their own. Well, those buildings might've been level, but the folk inside weren't level at all. They traded lies and whispers as much as goods there. Hell, maybe they were more valuable.

Nox parked his monowheel and strolled up the

sandy ramp to the city's easternmost gate, one of eight leading in and out of the metropolis. It was a trader's paradise, if there was any such thing as paradise in those parts, but you didn't get to set up shop without paying your rent. The Dust Barons might've turned a blind eye once you ponied up the cash, but until then those landlords were ever watchful. And Sam Silver, well, he didn't like to be watched, and he sure as hell didn't like to share his winnings. Well, *stealings* might've been a better word.

The gate was closed, which wasn't usual at all. The tollman perked up when he saw the Coilhunter. He pushed a long stick through the portcullis. It had a metal hand on the other end.

"A half," the tollman said, referring the toll. Half a coil was a lot to many, but he might've thought it wasn't much to the Coilhunter. Not with all those bounties he brought in.

"You sure 'bout that?" Nox asked.

"As sure as I am that you can afford it."

"It was a quarter not long back."

"And the Regime still existed not long back too. Things change, and change ain't good for … business confidence."

"Is that why the gates are shut? Beefin' up security?"

"Can't be too careful, Coilhunter."

"No, you can't."

But that begged the question. If the Dust Barons were being this careful now, how did Sam Silver get in unnoticed? How did he get to trade there without paying his dues? He sure as hell wasn't going to pay halfs.

Nox took a coil out of a pouch on his belt and snapped it in two along the scoured line. The Iron Empire considered that blasphemy, unless done by his sanctioned "breakers," as it had the image of the Iron Emperor on the back. They broke it in a way so as to preserve much of his visage across the separate parts, and only ever did it "for the good of spreading the will of the Iron Emperor," or so the breaker tomes said. But if you scoured it just right, you could make it snap his iron neck. For the superstitious out there, they'd say a few thousand people doing that every day must've contributed to his downfall. But Nox was there. He knew it took a whole lot more than snapping coins.

The tollman pulled the hand-stick in, added that half coil to the kitty, and opened the gate. "I take dollars too, y'know," he said, with that kind of smile that suggested he took pretty much any form of payment at all.

"You'll take whatever I give ya," Nox said as he strolled in.

The tollman nodded to himself. "You might've been wonderin' why we'd even let you inside in the first place."

"Well, now you weren't gonna stop me," Nox replied.

"Too right we weren't. We knew you'd get in somehow. At least this way we get you to pay your fare first."

"Ever the resourceful, those Dust Barons o' yours."

The tollman smiled again. "Ain't only half as resourceful as you."

Nox smiled back with his eyes and walked on. Then he halted as he passed the tollman, and his hand instinctively went for his hip. He saw something crawling up onto the tollman's shoulder. With that gunslinger speed he was known for, he clipped that scorpion before it had a chance to sting. The creature curled up in a ball on the ground.

"That … that was a pet," the tollman said.

Nox raised an eyebrow. "Well, you can put a gun to your head and call it a friend, but that don't make it so."

"Well, he cost me a quarter."

"Consider that a bargain then, because one of these days he might've cost ya your life."

And that was the thing the young didn't realise about the Wild North. You might've been bright-eyed when the sun rose and you thought it was smiling down at you, keeping you warm. You might've been bushy-tailed when you saw nature giving birth, thinking there ain't nothing better than the so-called "natural." You might've been broad-smiled when you saw the sand sculptures of the elders and the sandcastles of the young. But the sun was there to scald you. The scorpions were there to sting you. And the sand was there to drown you. Sooner or later, the sun or the scorpions or the sand would get you. All they needed was time.

Nox strolled on through the streets of the Burg, pulling his neckerchief up over his mask. It wasn't much of a disguise, he knew, especially with that familiar silhouette of his. There weren't many ways to hide a steel-plated guitar and oxygen tank.

The streets were packed, which helped. Everyone there was looking for something or selling something else. It was a do or die trade, with voices killing other voices. A woman selling dusters seemed to drown out the rest. And well, she did just fine.

Nox halted by a growing group of gossipers, who traded whispers like Sam Silver traded false dreams for coils. Those were the kinds of folk that got others into trouble, and right now the Coilhunter was hoping the one they were getting into trouble right now was Sam.

He donned an earpiece and cracked open a cylinder from his belt. Out came a mechanical moth in desert hues. It fluttered over to the crowd and landed on a nearby wall. The microphone inside picked up the voices loud and clear.

"You hear all this business with the Songsnatcher?" a man said.

"You mean the Coilhunter," a woman replied.

"It ain't him, Holly. It's someone new."

"Well, how do *you* know? They both wear a mask."

"I just know, Holly."

"It's him, I'm tellin' ya. Sure, doesn't he go by a thousand names?"

More people gathered, lured in by the horrid stories, completely oblivious to the Coilhunter standing nearby, cowled and covered up, with that neckerchief around his mouth, hiding the mask.

"I hear he's killin' 'im," one said. "The kids, that is."

"Cookin' 'im is what I heard."

"Ridiculous!" said a third. "He's usin' 'im for experiments. Secrets o' youth an' all."

"Vile stuff, that."

"I don't know 'bout that," another man said. "If they're demons, serves 'em right. I lost enough relatives in the war. They're the ones who started it, so they did. Took us to finish it. And if you ask me, we should finish 'em off for good!"

"I'm with ya there, John," an old woman said, as she pried her way into the conversation. "My daughter lost her baby when they came, and the next one she had wasn't really hers. Oh, and she knew it too. Kept tellin' me it throughout the pregnancy, but I wouldn't believe her. I didn't want to believe her. But she had a right dune-belly, she did. And that baby was born *wrong*. Knew it the moment I set eyes on 'im."

"Well, what did you do?"

"I told her to give 'im up, but she wouldn't have it. Said she fell in love with 'im when she saw 'im. I don't know how. He looked like us, mind you, but there was somethin' off. And lo and behold, when he was just six years old, he ratted her out to the Regime as a Resistance sympathiser. Right little demon, that boy."

"No wonder you moved up here," John said. "Some say it ain't safe, but at least we can make our own laws here. No need to bow down to the Regime *or* the Resistance. Sure, they're as bad as each other. I hear old Rommond's now a bit o' a demon-lover himself."

Nox sighed and rolled his eyes. It wasn't a crime to speak ill, or talk nonsense, or think foolish. Well, maybe more a crime of the mind. But that wasn't the Coilhunter's jurisdiction. He was there for the crimes of the hand, for the gunslingers and the headsmashers and the backstabbers. The crimes of the heart and the mind would have to wait. He didn't have enough space in the bounty box for them all. Well, you know what they said about the sun and the scorpions and the sand. Give it time, then. Give it time.

Chapter Seven

STOCKIN' UP

Nox wormed his way through the Burg, looking for those back alleys marked on Dozen-gun Dan's maps. It wasn't easy, because there were so many of them, and so many people in the way. There were quiet corridors here and there, sure, but they were quiet for a reason. Not everyone traded out in the open. Just the ones who wanted to live.

Nox walked down one of those dangerous streets, eyeing up the handful of people there coldly. Some of them froze mid-trade, one hand out for the money, the other hidden in a dark dust jacket. You had to be a gambler to trade there, because either they'd pull out that illicit substance you wanted or they'd pull out a gun. Some of them dealt in that demon-drug, Hope with a capital H, and others sold illegal photographs, a newer technology that was catching on fast. Of course, *illegal* was a matter of debate to most in the Wild North. Not to Nox.

He halted by one such trader and pulled down his neckerchief. Almost as soon as he did, he let out a black puff of smoke into the man's face. The buyer backed away slowly.

"I ain't here for you," Nox rasped. "But I could be.

And I will be, if ya don't tear those there pictures up."

The man gulped hard, but was otherwise frozen with fear.

"I don't hear any tearin," Nox continued. "That must mean you've got no use for those fingers o' yours."

The man's eyes widened and he quickly tore up the photographs and threw them on the ground.

"Smart boy," Nox said. "Let's hope ya stay that way."

Nox walked on, eyeing up the others as he pulled his neckerchief back up. Some of them wouldn't trade for days, he knew. That was a few days of cleaner streets. But he knew it wouldn't last. Even as he turned the corner, that photograph trader was piecing together the torn remnants. He'd tape them together for another trade. A quarter for a quarter. A half for a half. A full coil for the whole thing. And if you liked what you saw, you could pay a little more for the real thing.

When Nox reached an even quieter part of the back alleys, he glanced around to see that no one was watching. Then he launched one of the grapnels strapped to his arms and hauled himself up onto the roof of one of the buildings. From there he made his way across many others, then down again into a walled-off yard, which once belonged to a friendly acquaintance of his—now dead—and was now abandoned.

It was a tiny space, barely big enough to swing a criminal. But it was perfect for Nox. You see, that was where he hid some supplies. He could've gone back to his workshop in the Canyon Crescent, but that cost time. And time cost lives. This little restocking station would do just fine.

He grabbed the handle of a sweeping brush resting against one of the walls and gave it a good tug. With it came the wall itself, revealing a cabinet full of his old faithfuls. Container after container of blasting orbs and butterflies canisters. Row after row of shells and bullets. He even had one spare scarecrow mine, which he loaded into the latches at the bottom of his oxygen tank. He topped up the chemical mixture inside that too.

And there was something new to play with: a rocket pack that fitted around his oxygen canister, and strapped around his chest. He'd tested it before with one of his scarecrows, but he hadn't seen it in action himself. He hoped he'd never need it, but you didn't trust much in hope in the Wild North. You trusted in your guns. And if you were the Coilhunter, you trusted in your gadgets too.

Now that he was restocked, he closed the hidden wall, resting the sweeping brush back in place. Some folk said the Coilhunter would eventually run out. Some folk said his supplies had to eventually dry up. But like many folk who couldn't keep their yappers closed, they were all too wrong. You see, as long as there were bounties, there'd be bounty hunters. And as long as there was crime, there'd be the Coilhunter too.

Chapter Eight

THE NIGHT TRADE

Nox stayed on the rooftops for now, hopping across to others, watching the people as they moved about below. It was getting dark now, and the day traders changed over for their night equivalents. It was quieter trade in the darkness, which made it easier to spot people moving to and fro, if you could see them at all in the dark.

Nox pulled his night-vision goggles from his belt and slipped them on. He crouched on the edge of a building, scouting the streets. There were familiar figures down there, good and bad, and unfamiliar ones, who the Coilhunter knew he'd become familiar with soon enough. They went about their business, oblivious to the hunter perched on the rooftops. All they cared about was the trade. All Nox cared about was one particular trader.

It took another hour or so before he spotted Sam Silver's setup. He had three canopies covering his wares. His primary trade was those new "demon detectors" of his, small hand-held devices that purportedly told you who was human and who was one of those so-called "demons" of the Iron Empire. The Resistance might've called them simply the

Regime, and that regime might've fallen, but that didn't mean demand for knowledge of who was on either side fell with it. If anything, the welcoming of old Iron Empire folk into human society had brought out a resistance of another kind. Some didn't want to welcome them at all.

Nox watched for a moment to get a sense of Silver's customers. Most illicit trades had a certain kind of clientele, a stereotype, if you will. Maybe they were shifty like the gunrunners. Maybe they were shady like the sex traffickers. Maybe they were all shakes and shivers like the Hope-house dealers. Or maybe they weren't any particular kind at all, like those varied folk who strolled up to Sam Silver's stall. There were women and men, of all ages, shapes, and sizes. There were folk who looked like military, and others who were clearly farmers, and others yet who made a living—if you could call it a living—begging on the streets. All of them had saved up for these new inventions of Silver and his associates. All of them wanted to know who the demons were.

Nox could've leaped down and confronted Sam Silver right then and there, with not a guard in sight to stop him. But he felt a sudden unease. They say your gut's an animal that watched your back, and his gut was barking. Something about this catch, this kill, was too easy. The Wild North had a way of luring you in like that, like the mirage of an oasis on the horizon, deeper in the death-zone of the desert. You were either desert-wise or desert-dumb or desert-dead. Guess which one Nox was.

Now, Nox had encountered Sam Silver before,

and played his signature tune in a tone that was something frightening. You only had to hear it once for it to be embedded in your brain and emblazoned on your heart. You only wanted to hear it once, because the first time was bad enough. Sometimes you were left hearing phantom music as you worked and as you ate and as you dreamed. And, well, some only got to hear it once, and some never got to hear it at all. You couldn't quite say they were the lucky ones.

So, Nox pulled his steel-plated guitar from his back, his own bit of musical armour, and sat down on the edge of the roof, letting his legs dangle over the edge. He knew folk wouldn't quite see him in the dark, but they'd hear the twang of those guitar strings. Sam Silver would hear them the most.

He worked his fingers across those strings like lightning. It was a quick tune, but it was hauntingly distinct. It told of the journey across the desert. It told of the criminals running. And it told of the Coilhunter on the hunt. It told of the catch. And it told of the kill.

Sam Silver froze beneath the canopy. He let a coil slip from his fingers, where it rolled onto the ground, spun for a moment, then dropped dead just as the echoes of the Coilhunter's music faded. Silver looked up and out into the darkness, over to those black alleys, to those star-shunned streets. To that familiar silhouette that stalked the bad folks' dreams.

And then he ran, and so did his remaining now-panicking customers.

Nox wasn't the least bit surprised. After all, that's what the story of the music told. And remember what it told next. It told of the chase. Nox put his guitar away and ran right after him.

Chapter Nine

THE MUSIC OF THE CHASE

Nox was fast with a gun, but he was also fast on foot. He pelted through those streets and leaped right over the stall Sam had been trading at, diving feet-first under the shield of the canopy. He rolled on the other side, his guitar adding a little coda to his song.

He spotted the edge of Sam's white sleeve as he darted around the corner and quickly followed him, pulling out his right pistol as he ran. It was programmed into him to grab that weapon, just as it was programmed into Sam Silver to con every man, woman, and child he ever met. Folk said you could only ever do what God made you do. But God wasn't pulling the strings in the Wild North. The Devil was.

Nox pointed his gun around that corner before he threw the rest of him after it. It wasn't like the gun could see, but many a gunslinger would swear blind it could sense. It wasn't just cold iron. It was a part of you. Of course, some said a gunslinger was ninety-nine percent cold iron too.

Sam was gone. He'd turned another corner now, zig-zagging his way through the city's sandstone corridors. Nox went on after him, trying to make up their distance. He followed the clattering footsteps with his ears as much as he followed the fleeting glimpses of Sam's ivory clothing with his eyes. There weren't many folk who wore white like that in the desert, and there weren't many of them who were clean.

Nox's eagle eyes spotted a pile of crates ahead of him, stacked almost like a stairs. He bolted up them, grabbed the edge of the roof and hauled himself up, before he leaped down the other side, hot on the tail of the man in white. He halted and aimed a warning shot, clipping the edge of a building, but Silver kept running. There weren't many brave folk who'd do that, but there were plenty of fools. Nox had buried a lot of them.

The brief pause to line up that shot gave Silver an extra few seconds on his feet, but Nox had closed bigger distances in the past. He remembered the chase of Handcart Sally. And she was good. There wasn't much good about Sam Silver, except maybe that glistening garb of his. Quite the style alright. It'd look well on him in the grave.

Nox scaled the buildings again to get a better vantage, using one of his arm-strapped grapnel launchers to get onto the roof. He scoured the area, pulling out an eyeglass to see farther afield. It didn't take long to spot Sam Silver's distinctive garb two streets away. It wouldn't take long to get to him either.

Nox ran towards the edge of the roof, threw himself up and off, and extended his drifter wings with a sudden tug on a lever beneath his arm. He glided over to the next roof, where the wings folded back up neat and tidy as he landed. Then he dived down right on top of Sam Silver, dragging him to the ground.

They tussled and fought, and Nox got a bruised nose for his trouble, while Sam got a broken fist for his. You didn't go for the Coilhunter's face without risking hitting his mask. They fought again for a moment, Nox pinning one of Sam's arms, while Sam tried to reach for the Coilhunter's guns. Oh, he could have them alright. Well, the bullets anyway.

And then, as Nox forced Sam Silver onto his back, he got a real good look at the man's face, a face he knew quite well, and knew even better now from the Wanted poster. A face that should've been young and fair, and pretty—in so far as the Wild North let you be pretty. A face that should've been the one of a con artist, of a huckster and a trickster. But it was none of these. No, this wasn't Sam Silver at all, but it sure as hell was his clothes.

"You're not him," Nox said as he stood up and glanced around.

"Sure I am," the man said, and it wasn't Sam Silver's voice. "We all are."

That was when Nox saw it. There to the north, peeking out of one of the windows, was another man in that familiar white. There, to the east, gazing down provocatively from one of the rooftops, was yet another. There, to the west, were two more in similar attire, diving through the batwing doors of the local bar. They'd taken a leaf out of his book with his scarecrow Coilhunters, though these straw men walked and ran. All throughout the city there were dozens of "Sam Silvers," and somewhere amidst the decoys was the real deal, probably still dealing in his deceptive trade.

Nox took another glance at that Wanted poster with Sam's pretty face on it, taking in all the little features that the artist got so well. But this time Nox imagined a hundred of that man on that poster, and a hundred times the reward. It was just imagination, sure, but to all those fake convicts in his path, it would feel altogether real.

Chapter Ten

THE DANCE OF THE DECOYS

Nox didn't delay any longer. He fired his right grapnel at the man on the roof to the east, seizing him by the leg and pulling him down to the world below. Oh, you could pretend to be a god above, but the Coilhunter had a way of bringing you back down to earth with a crash. Hell, if God himself had a Wanted posted, Nox would fire that grapnel into the clouds.

As soon as that hook latched back into place, and Nox could see that his first Sam was a fake, he turned to his left and fell to his knee, casting a blasting orb like a bowling ball under the batwing doors of the saloon. He didn't need his blackout goggles for that, but the people inside sure wished they had them. The light from that orb made them temporarily blind. Yet that didn't stop two more fake Sams from stumbling out into plain view.

Nox took to the roofs, where he found another white-garbed Burgman taunting him. He dove right into the criminal and knocked him to the ground, before seeing it was yet another fake. The night gloom was doing him no favours, and the Burg's gaslights seemed to be dimmer than usual. The Dust Barons didn't do favours either—not unless you were paying for them, and paying more than their fair price.

Nox spotted another Burgman on the catwalks, doing a little fashion show in his suit of white. The Coilhunter swapped his real pistols for a set of fakes with rubber bullets. He wasn't one to name his guns, but if we were, he'd have called these his Sam Silvers. He lined up a shot and took out that strolling figure, and then another farther up, and two more patrolling below. They might've been guards. Hell, they might've been citizens. But if you were wearing that convict's clothes that night, you were almost certainly in on it, and you were lucky you wouldn't be in Sam's grave too.

Nox scoured the city, high and low, through the streets and through the buildings too. It wasn't the first time folk saw the Coilhunter in their living rooms or bedrooms, just like it wasn't the first time to see bandits and robbers there too. In the Wild North, your home was for your family, sure, but the lock on that front door was just a suggestion. The shutters on the windows were just for novelty too.

Nox had taken down close to two dozen fakes by now, and almost taken out a few others who just happened to be wearing something a little similar. Sure, they'd all come to soon enough, and maybe regret joining in this charade, but they'd regret it with a few bruises on their bodies and a few coils in their pockets. Nox wanted to know who put them there.

By now, he was approaching the dens of the Dust Barons themselves. In any other city, they would've built up real high, but they couldn't go too far up there, on account of the so-called architect's curse. Some folk said it was a Magus who did it. Some folk said it was done by the tribes. Some folk said that the land did it to itself. Well, some folk said that some folk had too much imagination. And some folk said that they had too little.

As Nox paused to survey the city from his new location, he couldn't help but sense a presence on a balcony above, and couldn't help but recognise the voice that wafted down to him, along with that ever-familiar stench of Rustport fish. Harvey the Hound.

"You," Harvey shouted down to him.

Nox repositioned to get a better view. He wasn't surprised to find the Hound barking out the window at a passer-by.

"Me," Nox rasped, "and a hundred Sam Silvers."

The Hound gave a roaring cackle. You could really hear the hyena in him. "Thought you'd get a kick outta that one."

"Not as much as the kick I'll give to the man who did it."

"Let me give you some advice," Harvey the Hound said. "For old times' sake. Give it up. You'll never find 'im. And even if you do, the city loves 'im. The cityfolk love 'im. So what if a few of his contraptions don't work the way he says they will. People want what he's sellin'."

"But he's sellin' dreams," Nox said.

"And people want dreams, Nox. People want dreams."

"Well, he's sellin' nightmares. Folk don't want those."

"No they don't," Harvey admitted. "That's why they don't want you."

A man came out onto the balcony behind the Hound and whispered in his ear. It was hard to see, as the night cowled him even more than Harvey, but it had the thin, tall shape of Grapevine Bill, the Hound's sycophantic servant.

"Well, Nox, a pleasure as always, but I gotta run," the Hound said.

"Your master throw your ball?" Nox taunted.

Harvey humphed. "Who says I have a master?"

"I find that every man who has a slave also has a master."

"And here I thought you didn't go in for philosophy. But Nox, I ain't got no slaves and I ain't got no master. I'm my own man. Like you."

"Funny, that. A lot of bad folk think they're like me."

"And what does that tell ya, huh?"

"That liars will lie, and robbers will rob, and dogs will bark. Let's hope you didn't bark up the wrong tree, *Harvey*. You might be up high now, but you're still in reach o' the pound."

The Hound laughed again. He waved his hand dismissively at the Coilhunter as he went back inside, before Grapevine Bill closed the doors behind him. Nox took an eyeglass glance through beforehand to see if the real Sam Silver was in there with them. He wasn't.

Nox spent another hour clearing out the city of decoys, and he began to wonder if Harvey was right that he wouldn't find who he was looking for. By this stage, the real Sam could've left the city altogether. But something felt off about this whole thing. No one would go through this much trouble to protect someone as low down the pecking order as Sam. This was bigger, and yet he couldn't understand why. He was starting to think that maybe this was just a distraction from the answer.

He was about to give up altogether when he retraced his steps. And there was the catch of the day—or make that the catch of the nigh—back at the place the Coilhunter first found him, under the canopy, selling wares from his stalls. Anyone else would've gone into hiding. But remember that Sam Silver was the brazen type. The brazen types never did learn their lessons easily. Well, as Nox approached Sam Silver from behind, you can remember one other thing: the Coilhunter was a good teacher.

Chapter Eleven

THAT WHICH SHIMMERS AIN'T ALL SILVER

"I should've known," Nox said, as he strolled up to Sam. This time the convict didn't run.

"You should have, yes," Sam Silver responded. "But we did give you quite the chase."

"I'll need to find out who this *we* o' yours is."

"I'd like to help you there, Coilhunter, but I just do what I'm told. I don't pay much attention to who's doing the telling."

"So long as they pay," Nox said.

Sam smiled. "So long as they pay."

"Funny, that," Nox croaked. "I'll make 'em pay too."

"Of that, I have no doubt," Sam replied. "But as for me, I'm innocent."

"Innocent of what?"

"Of whatever crime you've pegged me with."

"Then why did you run?"

"Well, *everyone* ran," Sam protested. "You tend to have that effect on people."

"Maybe, but not everyone has a whole lotta decoys for the chase."

"That, well … yes, that's different."

Nox circled the stalls, eyeing up the primary wares: those so-called "demon detector" devices. It was bad enough that folk would use them on each other, but some dune-belly dames would try them on their unborn children too. God only knows what they'd do then—and God didn't want that knowledge.

"They don't even work, do they?" Nox asked.

Sam Silver was about to speak, but he stopped himself. He bit his lip before attempting to answer again. "The fine print explicitly says they are for entertainment purposes only."

"Tell that to the men gunned down by their neighbours. Tell that to the kids hung by their parents. All for bein' so-called 'demons.'"

"The fine print also says that we accept no responsibility for how the product is used. And besides, Coilhunter, those are pretty everyday occurrences out here, if you haven't forgotten."

"I haven't forgotten," Nox said, "just like I haven't forgotten the warnin's I've given you before."

"I think you'll find that your warnings weren't very specific," Sam protested. "You should have, well, had some fine print."

Nox smiled with his eyes, as if he was waiting for a moment like that or a phrase like that. He slammed down the poster with Sam's face on it.

"That's some mighty fine print to me," he rasped.

"I … There must be some kind of mistake."

"There must be," Nox said. "The one you made that got ya on this poster. Or maybe the one that got ya caught."

"I'm a legitimate businessman, I *swear*."

"You might wanna think twice 'bout swearin' when there ain't no holy book to swear upon. But here, let me do ya one better. You could swear to God, with the penalty of his punishment in the afterlife. Or you could swear to me, and I'll punish ya in the here and now."

Sam Silver was nervous, but he wasn't lying about being a businessman. It was the *legitimate* part that didn't ring true. But Silver stayed professional, hiding the quiver of his lip behind some ever-confident words.

"I would gladly take your offer," he said. "And in return, you can, of course, sample my wares. I have many satisfied customers, I think you'll find— notwithstanding the odd unreliable, untrustworthy individual."

Nox scoffed. "I can see one odd, unreliable, untrustworthy individual already."

He picked up a few items from Silver's stalls, giving them a once-over. Most were junk, but they were genuine, even if the means by which Sam had procured them were likely questionable. Yet he also had some items that would appeal to a more discerning client. Tribal amulets and wardstones. Dreamcatchers and dayblessers. Not the usual trade for Sam Silver, but then he did tend to diversify a lot. You had to when you upset enough folks with the last lot you sold.

Then Nox turned his attention back to the main attraction: the demon detector devices, piled a dozen high in containers that hadn't already been emptied by the cityfolk. Nox pointed one at himself and waited for the reading. It was crudely made, with a dial on top, which could either point at the word *human* or *demon*, and a chunky badly-made button to set it in motion. He could hear the cogs working away noisily inside. Finally, it pointed at the word *demon*.

"Well, ain't that somethin'."

"It's not exactly *wrong*," Sam Silver explained. "I mean, when you look at it from a certain kind of perspective."

"You mean the perspective of a criminal?"

"Well, some do call you the Devil of the Desert."

"They call me a lotta things."

Sam pursed his lips to stop himself revealing that they called him some names he probably didn't want to hear.

Nox pointed the device at himself again and waited for another reading. This time it told him he was *human*. To some of the kids of the Wild North, that couldn't be true. For some of the criminals, that wasn't true either.

"Now, ain't that somethin' else," Nox said.

"It's … still a prototype."

"I don't see that in your *fine print*."

"Well, everything's a prototype. Like your gadgets. They're never the finished model."

"My gadgets do what they're supposed to."

"They haven't always, if you remember. And I see you testing new ones all the time."

"Yeah, but your gadget's a lie." Nox pulled apart the device and inspected the workings inside. From what he could tell, it was set up to give a random reading each time. "See. There ain't nothin' hear that could tell the nature of a man."

"I only sell folk what they want to buy," Sam Silver said. "What they want to see, what they want to hear. If they don't like their neighbour, if they suspect they're one of *them*, my product just gives them the confirmation they need—or want."

"You're givin' people a reason to kill each other."

Sam had to hold down a laugh. "Oh, Coilhunter, they really don't need one."

"I do," Nox said coolly. "And you're givin' me one."

"I think you'll find that with the Iron Empire gone, that Bounty Booth of yours isn't as well run as it once was. There just isn't the proper oversight anymore. They ran a tight ship, that Regime, maybe tighter than some under their care liked, but they at least verified that any claims of criminality were in fact true. That's why you could trust those posters before, Coilhunter." Sam Silver paused. "Can you honestly say you trust them now?"

Oh, he was good. He had the gift of the gab, that one. Some folk said a man like that could've talked the Grim Reaper into taking someone else instead. With all of Sam Silver's dangerous trade, Nox was pretty sure he'd probably sent the Grim Reaper after many already. But a good talker was one thing. A good bounty hunter was something else.

"I trust that you're an accomplice to a greater crime," Nox said.

"And what crime is that?"

"Snatchin' children from their homes."

"What proof do you have?"

"Funny you should say that," Nox rasped. He

unearthed a series of tiny photographs taken by his mechanical matchbox mouse, a tiny toy spy he'd used to get proof on a lot of criminals. "These prints are small, but the truth is big."

Sam Silver scrunched up his face and squinted at the images in Nox's gloved hands.

"I can't even see that," Sam Silver said.

Nox cast the photographs on the table, took a magnifying glass from his belt, and threw it on top of them.

"Better?"

"I still can't—"

Before he could finish, Nox grabbed the man and shoved his face down onto the table, his eye mere millimetres away from the magnifying glass.

"Now, don't you go tellin' me you still can't see, or I might get the impression there ain't no use for those peepers o' yours. And if there ain't no use for 'em, there ain't no point in you havin' 'em. So, boy. You want me to carve 'em out?"

"No! No! Please, Coilhunter!"

Oh, how they cried, and oh, how they pleaded. They were all brave at first, especially when they were with their gangs. But one by one, as Nox thinned them out, they turned to jelly. They were strong men until their knees buckled and their legs quivered. It didn't take much of an imagination to know what that did to their gun arms too.

"Now, boy," Nox said, pulling Sam Silver up so he could stare him straight in the eyes. "Tell me about this man that's grabbin' children from their cradles. The one the criminals like you say is as fast as me with a gun. The one they say is even faster with a singlestick. The one they're callin' the Songsnatcher."

Chapter Twelve

A SONG ABOUT
THE SNATCHER

Rumours of the Songsnatcher had been circulating around the Wild North for several weeks now, but so far the Coilhunter had yet to find him, or find anyone who had direct contact with him. He seemed to work alone, but then some evidence suggested he'd garnered support of some of the criminal underworld. Sam Silver seemed to be benefiting a lot from that arrangement.

"I don't know a lot about him," Sam Silver admitted.

"You know more than I do," Nox said. "Time to make that right."

"He wears a mask like you, except he covers all his face. You know, some folk say he *is* you, but I knew that was never the case. Some folk say he must be one of those Magi. Some folk say he was a slave who broke free of his master. Some folk say he's from tribal lands, on account of the music."

"Some folk should stop sayin' things," Nox mused. "But this music o' his. I heard tell it's somethin' mystical."

"An ancient tribal music," Sam shared. "Supposedly forbidden after the collapse of the Apanajo tribe, one of the oldest tribes, who were said to have been taught the first music."

"By the spirits," Nox said. "Yes, I've heard the tales."

"Well, there might be something in it. There's something powerful in that music, that's for sure."

"But why does it only work on children?"

Sam Silver shrugged. "Maybe it requires something that we've lost or forgotten. Maybe it requires belief and wonder. Maybe it requires innocence."

And that was the thing about the Wild North. It didn't just rob you of your innocence. It stopped the stagecoach of your life while it was just getting rolling and held you at gunpoint. If it didn't take your life, it took your youth and your looks and your health. And it'd be back again to halt your cart one final time.

"Or maybe," Sam continued, "it works on everyone, like all music does—just in different ways."

"Anything else?" the Coilhunter asked.

"Anything else we've lost since childhood? I can think of a few things, sure."

"Anything else you know about this snatcher?" Nox explained.

"Well, hmm, some folk say he was once your apprentice."

Nox cocked an eyebrow. "I ain't got no apprentices."

"That's what I said, but ... some folk don't listen to me."

"That's usually a good thing," Nox said. He paused. "These rumours ain't good for no one, but

I get it. When there's an information drought, you gotta make your own rain. And, well, you've only got yourself to blame when you get wet."

Sam Silver nodded in agreement. Yet it wasn't clear if he entirely agreed or was just humouring the Coilhunter, given his predicament.

"So," Nox said. "Tell me somethin' that ain't a rumour. Tell me what this Songsnatcher is up to now."

"He's planning something big," Sam Silver said. "I don't know the specifics—I swear I don't—but it has something to do with the Black Silk Collective."

"Those," Nox grumbled. He'd been on the hunt for them for years, but they were slippery—a little like Sam Silver was. They didn't just operate in the darkness. They operated as if they didn't exist. Past crime lords like Lawless Lyle had kept the crime gangs in line with fear, but the Black Silk Collective seemed to have an even deeper sway over people. Folk just didn't give them up. Or maybe folk just didn't know who to rat out. After all, they always wore masks.

"Do you know where I can find 'em?" Nox asked.

Silver might've laughed if he weren't so frightened. "No one does, except the buyer or the seller."

"And you've never been the buyer or the seller?"

"As I said before, Coilhunter, I'm a legitimate businessman. I don't go in for that kind of trade, even if the demand is good, and the money is better. I've got morals, you know."

"I don't know," Nox said. "I've seen you plenty, and seen your wares plenty more throughout the Wild North. Ain't ever seen your morals though."

"Well, I haven't seen your face," Sam Silver said,

nodding towards the Coilhunter's mask, "but just like the faces of the Black Silk Collective, I know it's there."

"Do ya now? Tell me something else you know."

"That's all I have on the Songsnatcher."

"And the Dust Barons?"

"Well, I know more about them, sure."

"I mean, do *they* know more about this snatcher?"

"Maybe, but I can't see them telling you."

"Oh, they'll tell me if I ask *real nice*."

Nox shoved Sam Silver back into his wares and turned to walk away. He paused and looked back over his shoulder.

"Consider this your final warnin'," the Coilhunter said. "If I so much as hear a whisper o' your name again, I'll come lookin', and I won't just give you a talkin' to. And don't you use that as a reason to go deal in the shadows more. I'll have the shadows watchin' too."

"I won't. I ... I'll be good," Sam Silver said.

"Now, don't you go makin' promises you know you can't keep. I ain't expectin' you to be *good*. I'm just warnin' you not to be *bad*."

"I won't," Sam said as he backed away. "I'll turn over a new leaf. I'll be a changed man."

Nox wasn't so sure he could believe that. His old friend Chance Oakley might've believed in second chances, but more often than not the only change the Coilhunter saw was when the good folk went bad, and the bad folk got worse.

"Wait," Nox said, before he took that demon detector out of a pouch on his belt. He pointed it at Sam Silver and thumbed the button. The dial shifted for a moment before pointing at the word *demon*. "Well, whaddya know. Maybe it works after all."

Chapter Thirteen

THE BLACK SILK COLLECTIVE

It was an undisclosed location. That was how the Black Silk Collective operated. You never saw them under the street lights of the Burg. You never saw them guzzling beer at the saloons. You never even saw their faces or knew their names. They were known by a codename only, and you only ever knew the codenames of a few. You worked in small numbers so you could die in small numbers. They were decentralised, with no known leadership, though some suspected there was one behind the silk-covered scenes.

Oh, they wore masks too. Black silk veils hanging from black, cat-eared, felt glasses. You might've thought they were there for a masquerade, but they weren't there for a costumed dance. They were there to do ugly, dark things—things that no amount of pretty lace masks could hide.

Several of the masked figures unloaded a land-ship-treaded troop carrier, like something you'd see in the war down south, when that war was raging. Many of those vehicles had been repurposed for other ends, and some had fallen into nefarious hands.

The Black Silk Collective fuelled the brothels

and bars across the Wild North, and even had "missionaries" who went into southern territory to expand their influence. And they did it with women, and they did it with children too.

This latest convoy contained girls from ages five to ten, all born after the time of the Harvest, that fateful moment when the Iron Empire invaded the world of Altadas. That meant they were, as many viewed them, demon spawn put there by those invading forces. Some folk said they did it with magic. Some folk said they used advanced technology instead. Some folk said they did nothing at all, and it was just propaganda by the Resistance. It didn't matter. Enough believed it to hand over their children to the Black Silk Collective willingly. And for those who weren't willing, the Collective had other means of encouragement.

"Are these all for the Burg?" one man asked. He scratched at his nose, where his mask was making a dent. Unsurprisingly, they called him Billy the Itch.

"Only two dozen," a woman replied. "The rest are a Night Slaver restock for the regulars. Black Lilly has a map of the drop-offs. We're gonna be travellin' a lot tonight."

"Thought I was gonna get to go home early," Billy the Itch said. "The wife's been callin' me Old Neglectful. Has the kids sayin' it too."

"You've already got a *silk-sign*," the woman said. "But you best not tell me any more or I'll know who you are beneath."

"I'm not the only family man here, Ida Ninetails," Billy the Itch protested. "There's Gutless Gabe and

Ernest White-eyes, for a start."

"And let's finish it there," Ida Ninetails said, "or someone'll finish you."

"Speakin' of," Black Lilly said, as she drew up close with the map. She rolled it up hurriedly and shoved it down her top. "Who's that out there in the dark?" She pointed towards a figure riding slowly towards them. You could barely see him, just like you could barely see them. But he spotted them alright, long before they'd spotted him.

"There's no drop-offs here, is there?" Billy the Itch asked. "I thought this was just a collection spot."

"It is," Black Lilly said. "You go scare 'im away."

"I ain't the scarin' type!" Billy the Itch said. "Get Gabe to do it."

But Gabe didn't do it, and neither did the rest of them. Instead, the figure drew closer, and the girls that had yet to be loaded onto the truck all turned their heads towards him.

"It's the Coilhunter!" some of them shouted. The relief was audible in their cries.

Yet just as they cheered, the shadow came closer, and in that silhouette you could see the shape of a gun.

Then a man's voice, muffled by a mask, but it didn't quite sound like the Coilhunter. "Little birds, little birds, how you do sing."

And they sung alright. And they screamed. And then the gunfire died down as all those little chirps cut out. The shells dropped with the bodies. And the Songsnatcher struck again.

Chapter Fourteen

THE DEAD'S BREADCRUMBS

It didn't take long to track down the destroyed carrier. Nox didn't need to scour the sand for tracks. He saw the smoking ruins of the truck from a mile away.

He saw the bodies too as he pulled up. It looked like some of them ran. It looked like some of them ducked for cover. But you can't outrun bullets. And you can't hide in the empty wastes of the desert. That didn't leave many options. You could perish or die or kick that old tin bucket. Quite the choice there.

Nox shook his head as he passed body after body. They were all just children. It wasn't the first massacre like this he'd found. Each one numbed you a little, but it never numbed you enough. It hardened your heart and broke it at the same time.

He stopped to stare down at a seven-year-old girl, whose eyes were still wide open—now eternally so. He wanted to know what she knew before she passed. He wanted to see who she saw before her life was snuffed out. Who was this man who hated them so much? Their only sin was being too young. Their only crime was that they were children. If they'd been sixteen or seventeen, born after the Harvest, no one would've ever called them "demons." No one would've ever called for them to be culled, for them to be killed.

It brought back memories of his own children, killed so long ago, and yet so recently. Little Ambrose, gentle and resourceful, and little Aaron, wild and wonderful. They too were young, so young, and born after the Harvest. But there was no demon in them. Nox was sure of that. If the Iron Empire had ever managed to control the birth channels of the entire population, to ensure that humans gave birth to *maran* people—as they were ultimately called—then it didn't matter much to Nox. They were still kids. And, as far as he was concerned, they were still his. He loved them, and they loved him. He knew that with every fibre of his being. He knew it at the core of him. He knew it in his heart.

Thinking of his family now only angered him. Looking at all those other folk's families strewn across the desert only angered him more. This wasn't just an attack on them. It was an attack on him. It was an attack on everything he stood for, everything he fought for. He was the self-made sheriff of the Wild North, and he had his own painted-on badge to prove it. He'd hunt down that killer. It wasn't just a promise made by him. It was a promise made by all the other wrongdoers he'd hunted down before.

Nox halted suddenly, his gun already drawn. He held it low at his hip, resting it there to steady his arm, his blue coat pushed back behind him. He thought he'd heard something. Maybe footsteps. That wasn't a sound you wanted to hear in a graveyard, unless it was the dead marching to their graves. Or it was the person who sent them there.

"Well, look who the sandworm spat out," a voice said from behind him.

Nox turned his gun before he turned the rest of him. If he'd heard the click of a trigger, he would've fired before he even saw the target. And you bet your ass he would've hit.

It was lucky for Johnny Grin, standing there across the way, that Nox was just as good at holding back his trigger finger as he was at letting it loose.

"Johnny Grin," Nox said, as if he was the sandworm doing the spitting now.

"The one and only," Johnny replied. "Not like you, Coilhunter. Heard tell there's another o' ya out there, roamin' the wastes. Looks like he did a number on these girls here."

"What are ya doin' here, Johnny?"

"Same thing as you, I'm guessin'. Trackin' down that Songsnatcher. Did ya know they increased the reward? Oh, of course you do. You're in it for the money, just like the rest o' us. But see, I thought you were after Sam Silver. Did you not catch your little fish?"

"I caught 'im alright, and he led me here."

Johnny Grin gave his trademark smile. "Good for you, Coilhunter, good for you." He shrugged. "I guess *I* didn't need the detour."

Nox grumbled to himself, but tried to keep it low. That was hard, because his mask echoed out the noise along with another of his ceremonial puffs of black smoke. Some folk said the chemical mixture he inhaled was doing as much damage to him as the desert air. Some folk said he added the smoke just for effect. Some folk said it was what devils breathed out. Those folk were likely the same ones who believed the children were demons. Nox'd have to pay those folk a visit and see what else they said.

Johnny Grin sauntered up to the Coilhunter. He was the kind of man who couldn't help but swagger. He would've swaggered to the altar and swaggered to the grave. There were folk like that who Nox had helped along their way.

"So, what've ya got?" Johnny Grin asked him.

"Nothin' for you, that's for sure."

"Oh, don't be like that, Coilhunter. We could saddle up and solve this one together, you and I."

Nox glanced at him and raised an eyebrow. "We ain't partners."

"I know, I know. You're a 'lone wolf' and all that. I heard ya howlin'. Must get tiresome though."

"Somethin's tiresome, yeah."

Johnny Grin took no heed. That was the trouble with folk like him. They didn't pay enough attention to be afraid. That was dangerous for others, but also dangerous for themselves. Fear had a purpose. It kept you safe. In the Wild North, you didn't live. You lived afraid.

"Doesn't look like much to go on," Johnny Grin said, as he kicked over one of the bodies.

Nox grabbed his shoulder. "Have some respect for the dead."

Johnny Grin's eyes were wide. "You usually don't."

"For the victims, I do."

Johnny Grin reached down and held the cheeks of one of the girls. "Don't ya wish you could hear 'em? Let 'em tell ya who did it. It'd be easier then. A quicker buck is a better buck, I always say." He shook the girl's head, as if she disagreed. "She ain't sayin' nothin'."

Nox grumbled more audibly, but Johnny Grin ignored him. He dusted some footprints by one of the older girls, who looked like she'd tried to shield the others and run for her attacker. She'd gotten close, but close meant as much as far away when you were dead.

"You're messin' up those prints more than uncoverin' 'em," Nox observed. It looked like Johnny Grin had hubris by the measure, but not a lot of sense or training. That was the trouble with those new bounty hunters. They wanted the money, sure, but they didn't want to pay to learn how to get it. And why would they, when they could rob and launder like the rest of them. Nox had hunted bounty hunters as much as he'd hunted their quarry.

Nox stopped suddenly as his boot clipped something in the sand. He looked down to see what appeared to be a large hardback book, half-buried. To some folk in distant lands, that might not have meant much at all. But to those in Altadas, that meant everything. You see, the Iron Empire had outlawed literature, and that meant many would-be readers went up north for their illicit hobby. It wasn't just criminals that fled to the Wild North. Those who enjoyed culture had little option but to follow suit.

Yet, even then, books were rare enough in the Wild North, and those who could read them were rarer still. This was a clue, no doubt about it. What it pointed to wasn't yet clear.

Nox took up the book and turned it over to inspect the title. *The Self-Made Miner* was the name, written by a Wallace Wickaby, SMM. Those latter initials presumably stood for Self-Made Miner and were probably just as made-up as the content of the book itself. A cursory glance showed wild ideas about where you'd find gold, with every instance of the word "gold" crossed out and replaced in handwriting with the word "iron." That meant it must've been written before the Harvest, and "edited" some time after, when the Iron Empire ensured there was only one metal worth having. The "instant riches" promised in Wickaby's writing read like something Sam Silver would've gone in for—or something Sam Silver might've written himself.

"What've ya got there?" Johnny Grin asked, peering over his shoulder. "So, they're a lettered type, huh?"

"Depends who *they* are," Nox said. It could've just as easily belonged to someone in the Black Silk Collective as to the Songsnatcher himself. By the Coilhunter's logic, it wasn't likely a killer would pause to read a chapter, but then folk had done stranger things in the Wild North. Some might've said he was one of them.

Nox thumbed through the pages, fighting off Johnny Grin's hands as he tried to turn back to the one before. Then the Coilhunter rested on the bookplate on the inside cover, which told him exactly where the book came from: *Ex Libris The Bookspine Saloon.*

And it told Johnny Grin the same.

"Race ya," Johnny Grin said before he darted off to his three-wheel motorcycle, known around those parts as a hyper-hog, which he'd parked right beside the Coilhunter's monowheel.

Nox shook his head and walked on up to his vehicle as Johnny Grin sped away. He didn't like the idea of a race with that other bounty hunter at all. Not because he thought he wouldn't win, but because he knew Johnny Grin would just get in the way. The last thing you wanted in a gunfight was other folk passing through.

Nox got into his monowheel and started the engine. It spluttered and coughed, and Nox knew instantly that it wasn't just from the desert sand. He glanced around at the fuel tank, which had a big old hole in the side. The diesel leaked out like blood all around it.

So, scratch that. The last thing you wanted in a gunfight was someone stabbing you in the back while you took aim.

Chapter Fifteen

DIESEL DROUGHT

Nox patched up the tank as best he could, sealing the hole, but it was clear there wasn't a whole lot of diesel left. Even the spare canister was gone. You had to be brave or crazy to do that to the Coilhunter's vehicle. There were a lot of brave and crazy faces on Wanted posters, and quite a few more braving the dirt six feet below.

Nox took a device from his belt and stabbed the sand with it. It had a kind of straw on one end and a suction system on the other, drawing up whatever moisture was there. It wasn't perfect, but you didn't need perfect to survive in the Wild North. You needed anything you could get your sun-blistered, sandpapered fingers on.

Nox held up the little clear canister and sloshed the diesel around inside. It wasn't much, but it was better than letting the desert have it. Some folk said the desert was just as thirsty as you were, and that you ought to have mercy on it. Well, those folk needed a reminder—and they often got it—that the desert had no mercy for you. It'd slurp you right up if it could, and cough out the bones.

Nox knew he wouldn't get all the way to the

73

Bookspine Saloon with what little diesel he had left. He needed a top-up, and there weren't many places around those parts where you could get it. The Roaming Oasis had some, sure, but you'd be as lucky to stumble on that as water itself. The Burg had some, double sure, at the Dust Barron's double prices, but he didn't think he'd have enough juice to get there.

Nox inspected the overturned truck for fuel, but it was clear that it'd been bled dry long before. If it wasn't the Songsnatcher, it'd have been Johnny Grin. And if it wasn't Johnny Grin, it'd have been any number of other scavengers that saw the smoking ruins on the horizon—a beacon to the needy and a lighthouse to those who had unquenchable needs.

Nox had two options: he could send up a flare and wait it out to see if a kind passer-by would lend his corpse some fuel, or he could call in a little mechanical aid. He chose the latter, dialling a few buttons on his wristpad. Less than an hour later, a large wind-up eagle, sent by Oddcopper in his workshop, flew overhead. It lowered down a half-can of diesel on a grappling hook, which Nox used to top up his newly-patched tank.

He gave a nod to that eagle as it flew away, as if it were the real thing. They were just toys at one time, but to the kids who played with them, they were as good as real. Nox'd lost his kids, but he'd kept alive that part of him. In the empty wastes of the desert, it paid to have a little imagination.

Nox pulled the edge on his map-watch, which rolled out a map of the area. If he'd kept pulling, he could've seen the parts off the map too—the places the old mapmakers used to mark as "here be monsters." The cartographers of the Wild North could've marked that anywhere.

Once Nox had gotten his bearings, he drove off, a little slower than usual to conserve his fuel. It was topped up for now, sure, but burning rubber only got you places if you had rubber to burn.

He travelled a few hours, watching the tracks and watching the snakes slithering new ones. And there it was in the distance, that destination for the well-quenched and the well-read: the Bookspine Saloon.

Chapter Sixteen

THE BOOKSPINE SALOON

The Bookspine Saloon earned its name from those batwing doors that were moulded into the shape of books. When you pushed on through them, it was as if you were turning pages. And there was an added beauty in the fact that the owner, Peggy "The Librarian" Cassidy, had more than a dozen of those book-doors made, so she could alternate them to represent a different favoured book of hers. That day's title was *The Watering Hole* by Annie Westwood, an old classic of the world of Altadas from when there was a lot more water and a lot more readers too. The extra applicability to the saloon didn't hurt either.

When Nox entered, he found Johnny Grin already in there, slurping down some tangleleg at the bar. Nox sighed heavily and let his boots carry the sound a little more with some well-placed stomps— and his legs were anything but tangled. The room's eyes turned to him. The room's guns turned to him beneath the tables too. You see, there was something you learned quick about the folk who frequented the Bookspine Saloon. They were willing to die to defend their literature. That was perhaps a good thing, because for so long the Iron Empire was willing to kill them.

Nox approached the bar and gestured for a drink. Peggy Cassidy didn't need to ask what drink, because most folk knew that the Coilhunter was partial to some old orchard. Of course, some folk said he drank blood too. And Nox let them say it.

"And what else are ya havin'?" Peggy Cassidy asked him. "You sure as sand ain't just here for the neck oil."

"I already asked her," Johnny Grin said, with a neck that seemed well-lubricated.

"And I already answered," Peggy replied, "assumin' you're talkin' 'bout that book ya found."

"*The Self-Made Miner*," Nox said, placing the title on the counter.

"Just like the self-made sheriff," Peggy said. "And a self-made gentleman for bringin' this back to this here culture cache. I like to think of our books like sheep, with me their shepherd."

"Well, ya lost one," Johnny Grin interjected.

"Who was it lent to?" the Coilhunter asked.

"I checked the ledger for this barfly here," Peggy said, before pulling up her records from behind the bar. She had a wooden bookmark holding open a page. "One Black Lilly."

Johnny Grin nudged the Coilhunter. "Another race?"

Nox glared at him. "Put another hole in my tank and I'll put a hole in your head."

"That's fair," Johnny admitted. "What'll you do if I break your axle?"

Nox's voice grew even grittier. "Guess."

Johnny Grin cocked his head. "Well, let's hunt her without the gimmicks, then."

"You don't need to hunt me," a voice came from across the room. "I'm here."

Chapter Seventeen

AIN'T DEATH JUST
ANOTHER BEDTIME

Up in Oldtown, the townsfolk were settling in for another good night of the old restful. The horses had been fed. The kids had been fed. The men from the mines had been fed. There was nothing like a good meal to send you off to a peaceful slumber.

The last lights went out an hour or two after dusk. This was summertime, but it wasn't like you really knew the difference in the Wild North. Spring was warm. Summer was scalding. Fall was hot. Winter was sweltering. If anything, summer was more a punishment than a prize, because those longer days meant longer hours of that oh so unforgiving sun. Don't think it'd forgotten the curses you had for it either. Why, it cursed you right back.

Oldtown was quiet in recent months, after the Coilhunter'd sent a "duck patrol" through. You'd think by now the criminals would know they weren't all carrying eyeblinders and explosives, but it wasn't even just that. Where there was a toy duck, the Coilhunter wasn't far behind. Some of those folks were gamblers, but they didn't dare gamble on that.

But that familiar quiet of the town, well, it helped

you sleep. Hell, you could barely hear the far-off howls of the dust coyotes. No, you were more likely to hear your house creak, or your papa snore, or your momma prepping food for tomorrow's breakfast. And those were reassuring sounds. The sounds of the home. The sounds of safety.

But there was a different sound on the wind that night. It sounded like a flute, wooden and hollow, but with an echo you'd be hard-pressed to mimic in deep-dug valleys. That canyon-carried reverberation played instead across the plains, and if you could strain your ears to hear it, you might've had to press your ear against the barrier to the world hereafter.

The children dozed soundly, even when they stirred from their beds, even when they threw off their bedclothes and placed their tiny feet into their tiny slippers. The children dozed soundly, even when they stood upright, even when they wrapped their nightcoats around their shoulders and tied the fastenings like a lasso around their waists. The children dozed soundly, even when they stepped gently across the creaking floorboards, even when they grabbed the handles of their doors and walked outside. The children dozed soundly, even as they all left behind the sounds of safety and followed instead that ethereal music into the darkness of the desert night.

Chapter Eighteen

BLACK LILLY

Peggy Cassidy gave the Coilhunter, Johnny Grin, and Black Lilly one of the back rooms of the Bookspine Saloon. Unsurprisingly, it was a room filled wall-to-wall with books. Even the furniture was covered with them, forcing Nox to remove a huge stack just to sit down.

"I want to know everything," he said. "Every detail you can remember."

"Assumin' you ain't the Songsnatcher," Johnny Grin added.

Nox nodded slowly. "Assumin' that."

"Well, I ain't the Songsnatcher, I'll swear that on the sand," Black Lilly said.

"The sand ain't much for swearin'," Nox replied.

"How about on a booklover's books then?"

"Well, that at least means somethin'."

"Never been much of a reader myself," Johnny Grin said, as he cast a few tomes away carelessly and sat down on a pile of others. Black Lilly grumbled audibly, so you could tell it meant more than a little to her.

"How'd you escape?" Nox asked her.

"I crawled under the truck as soon as the first

bullets fired."

"You didn't think to protect the children?"

"I thought to protect myself."

"Smart girl," Johnny Grin said as he lounged back. "That's what I would've done."

Nox didn't doubt it.

"He gunned those girls down before anyone could do anything."

"And if he hadn't … would they have done anything?" Nox asked.

"I'll be real with you, Coilhunter. Probably not. Girls like that are a quarter coil a dozen. We'd cut our losses and recoup 'em elsewhere."

"*We* bein' the Black Silk Collective, huh?"

"You know I can't comment on that."

"Well, you better comment on somethin', 'cause this Songsnatcher needs to be caught."

"He was masked up like you, but had goggles over his eyes. His garb was darker though, closer to black, but with a stark white belt. His hat might've been different too, a bolero I think, with a band of white as well. The arms of his duster had white bands too, if I remember right. He was a gunslinger, that was for sure. He barely moved as he gunned 'em down."

"Is that all?" Nox asked. "Did ya see where he went? What vehicle he used?"

"He rode a horse, a black stallion with a white mane and white featherin'. Shucks, that seems to be his whole motif. The Man with the White Stripes. That's what we'd call 'im if he were you."

"Well, he ain't me, is he?"

"Jury's out on that one," Johnny Grin said, as he

sliced an apple and ate a piece with the blade.

"Oh, I've no doubt now," Black Lilly said. "I wondered about the rumours at first, but he was nothin' like you. There was no gadgets. No flair."

"Flair," Johnny Grin said. "I knew I had a word for ya."

Nox ignored him. "Where'd he go? We didn't see any horse tracks back there."

"That might be 'cause his horse was tied up across the dunes. I followed 'im a little and spied 'im with my eyeglass. I think he knew I was followin' too, but he paid no heed to me. It was just the girls he was after."

"The kids," Nox grumbled.

"Look, I know you think what we do with 'em is cruel, Coilhunter, but we give 'em work."

"You make 'em slaves."

"They get fed. They get housed. They get bathed."

"Only 'cause they get *used*."

"It's a better life than some out here. And it's better than bein' dead."

Nox had no answer to that. He'd vowed to one day take down the Black Silk Collective, and those who supplied them, but he knew it wasn't all black and white. In the Wild North, freedom meant nothing if you had no food to eat. It wasn't right, but not much was. Nox was hoping to change that, one day at a time, one bounty at a time.

"So where'd he go?" Nox asked.

"He headed north, towards tribal territory. I half-wondered if he was from those tribes, but I didn't want to seem, well, hidebound. I ain't usually known to be bigot."

"No," Nox said. "Just a slaver. Funny, that."

"Do you want this information or what?"

"Go on," Nox grumbled. He wanted to do more than grumble, but there were bigger fish to fry, and he was thinking of a bigger fire.

"He seemed to meet up with a group o' bandoleros, all in his trademark black, but without the stripes. They formed a posse and went on into old Apanajo lands. You know, the Cactus Wastes."

"I know 'em."

"I don't," Johnny Grin said. "Except by name."

"Folk say it's just endless cactus fields, as far as the eye can see. Not much else up there."

"Except the Songsnatcher," Nox said.

"Well, then," Johnny Grin said. "Let's saddle up, cowboy."

Chapter Nineteen

A LITTLE LESSON IN MANNERS

Now, Johnny Grin might've learned his lesson about punching holes in the Coilhunter's monowheel tank, but Nox knew more than most that the bad folk of the Wild North didn't learn easy. It was one thing to warn them. It was quite another to teach them.

As Johnny Grin darted out the door, trying to get that upper hand again, Nox pulled a compact grenade gun from his belt and aimed it right at the bounty hunter's heels. When he fired, the other folk in the saloon scrambled away for safety, but it didn't launch an explosive shell. Instead, it sent an egg-shaped orb, which cracked open mid-air, revealing an ever-expanding toy snake. Johnny Grin must've heard the noise behind him, because he glanced back just in time to see that slithering creature fly through the air and wrap around his lower legs. He tripped forward with a thud, and the snake expanded around his torso, pinning his arms as well.

"That's not fair," Johnny Grin said, struggling to say it as his head pressed against the sand.

"That ain't a *thank ya*, and it should be. You're lucky it ain't a bullet."

Johnny Grin didn't protest too much at that. He squirmed and struggled, but it seemed the more he fought, the tighter the snake-trap became.

Nox strolled right past him, placing one of those big old, many-buckled boots of his right down by Johnny Grin's face. You could walk all over the good folk of the world, but sooner or later, they'd don boots of their own. And you sure as hell hoped they weren't wearing spurs.

Nox got on his monowheel, turned it, and revved loudly. He tapped the side the tank, where he'd patched up the hole. Johnny Grin looked up sheepishly, and kept on looking, and kept on struggling, as the Coilhunter rolled away.

Chapter Twenty

THE CACTUS WASTES

It was a long journey north, but then most journeys were long in the Wild North. The towns were few and far between, and the desert's features were fewer and farther. He was glad he was topped up on fuel now, because you didn't want to get stuck out there in the emptiness.

The Apanajo lands were visible clearly on the horizon. The periodic, spartan placement of cacti, which the Wild North knew well, changed suddenly into an impenetrable wall of them, almost as if nature had finally learned how to keep man out.

Nox pulled up close, but left his monowheel outside. It was clear that this was a boundary, and though he wasn't one for the spiritual, you couldn't help but feel you needed to honour the land there. A diesel-guzzling, smoke-spewing machine didn't quite say honour, that's for sure. Except maybe to the biker gangs.

The cactus fields went on for miles, and that was no exaggeration. They lined the horizon and crowded the foreground. They clustered together tightly in places and spread out widely in others. Some were familiar shapes and sizes, while others were tiny bulbous plants, and others still were towering titans, several times the height of man. Some were safe, with edible cactus pads and drinkable water stored inside. Others were poisonous, with some that would cause you to hallucinate, and others that would do you in, drying your insides out even faster than the stalking sun.

Nox walked between and amongst them, awed by the beauty and majesty of some, and disgusted by the twisted and tormented forms of others. Those fields had everything, like a hundred thousand people assembled. There were good ones and there were bad ones. And there were rotten ones, badder than bad, deadlier than death.

This was the land of the Apanajo, and even here in the emptiness you could hear the echo of a song. The whistle of the wind was like the voice of an ancestor. The shifting of the spine-trees was like a dance. And yet all of that spoke of memory, of the long-forgotten and the never-was. It spoke of past things and past people, and yet there was the land of the present, unused but by nature, yet still haunted by the footfalls of those who came before.

Nox had wondered in the past why no one else had claimed those lands, but now he knew the answer. It *was* claimed. It was always claimed. It was claimed by nature and claimed by the Apanajo still. To walk there was to walk among them, and to live there was to invite madness, for you could never ever escape the song.

Nox was so mesmerised by the landscape that he started to forget why he was there. He wondered if those handful of folk who went there for their own reasons ended up the same way, wandering until their end of days—or maybe wandering there still.

And that was when one of the cacti moved.

Nox heard it, and knew it wasn't just the rustle of nature. He turned sharply to see what this new threat of flora was.

And that was when the cactus fired.

Chapter Twenty-one

SHADOWS AND SHARPSHOOTERS

Nox dived low, narrowly missing the incoming bullet. He scrambled through the brush, his eyes darting from side to side to find cover, and also to find where the attackers were hidden. He knew there was more than just one of them, because he'd heard two guns fire, and he sure as hell hadn't hit the trigger. He'd only just about hit the deck.

He found some cover behind a tightly-packed cluster of angel wings cacti and peered through the cactus pads to scout out his assailants. They'd gone quiet now, as if they just had one shot each, but you'd be a fool to believe that. There were more bullets in the Wild North than folk to put them in. Nox had a belt full of his own.

He scoured the Cactus Wastes, focusing on where he'd thought the bullets came from, but there was nothing out there but more desert plants. Some of them weren't much by way of cover, and those that were had just the one flora-shaped shadow. The sun betrayed all eventually, but right now it didn't betray those sharpshooters. Nox hid in the shade of his own cactus cover, but the way the sun was pointing, there just couldn't be anyone out there who didn't cast a giveaway shadow of their own. There was something odd about this. They had him at a disadvantage, whoever *they* were. Unless it was the cacti themselves who'd taken up arms. Well, stranger things had happened in the Wild North.

Nox took his guitar off as gentle as he could, careful not the strum the strings. The wind whistled by just in time, hoping to catch a note and send it to all waiting ears. You see, the wind didn't care if the sun saved you for later. It'd out you right here and now, while the going was good, and the guns were ready. But Nox knew that wind, and knew those strings, and knew even the sand he placed the guitar down upon. He flicked a switch on the instrument, which started the release of a thick smoke, then slid it as far as he could to one side.

The bullets came, fast and sudden, pelting off the metal chassis of the Coilhunter's fabled guitar, and off the nearby cacti, which shook like dummies in a practice range. Nox peered again through the cactus pads, watching the hail of bullets that came from two, no, three directions. An extra gunman had joined in this time, and not one of them spared their ammo. Yet not one of them gave up their location either. The bullets came from the cacti, but there were no hands visible, no heads poking over the top, no shuffle of feet below. These weren't just gunmen. They were ghosts.

The gunfire died down, and so did the smoke, revealing Nox's sun-shimmering guitar out in the open, and half a dozen cacti blown to bits, and half a dozen more riddled with bullet holes. You could've said *someone wanted him dead*, but that didn't mean a lot in the Wild North. A lot of *someones* wanted him dead. They just usually were a little more visible when they made their feelings known.

Nox needed to get closer, but he didn't figure his chances were a whole lot better than those destroyed cacti. Those gunmen were snipers, and they were ready for him. It made him wonder if the Songsnatcher was up here at all or if he'd just been sent into a trap. For all he knew, that snatcher was half a desert away, adding to his collection while Nox was kept busy in those cactus fields.

The sun was shifting, moving the shadow of his cactus cover ever so slightly. Nox moved a little with it, so his own shadow stayed in sync. If he wasn't careful, and he didn't move in step with the sun, he'd be outed there to the three sharpshooters just waiting to shoot him sharp. Yet, if he waited long enough, he'd be forced to move right out into the open to keep his shadow in check—and it seemed like those gunmen were happy to wait that long. Nox would've been too if he was the hunter. He sure as hell didn't like being prey.

The Coilhunter had a few choices open to him: he could run out, all guns blazing, but at least half of those guns would be blazing his way; he could try to even out the odds with some gadgets, maybe something that could scout the way for him, but that could reveal his location just as easily; or he could call in the cavalry and mow down some of those cacti and whoever was behind them. Maybe the spirits of the ancestors wouldn't like that last option, but surely they didn't like a gunfight on their sacred ground, and they weren't doing anything about that. Unless, of course, they were the ones doing the shooting. Either way, the cavalry was sounding pretty good right now.

Nox crouched down low and dialled a few buttons on his wristpad. He cupped it under his arm to hide any small sounds. The wind was back, begging for another chance to betray him. It could beg all it wanted. Some day, when the wind itself was on a poster, he'd make it beg some more.

Nothing happened for a moment, except one more tick of the sun's clock, and one accompanying shift of the shadows, and Nox's own nudge towards the open.

Then there was the far-off hum of an engine, and then a growing rumble, and then a sudden roar as the Coilhunter's monowheel, now in automation mode, trundled through the cactus fields, clipping the arms off the desert fruit as it passed. It raced past Nox's position, bowling down a few of the smaller plants in its path, and kept on going.

The bullets came next, pelting off the vehicle, blowing another hole in the tank. If that was Johnny Grin out there, back for round two, well, Nox had two rounds in the chamber to make things even.

Nox ran out from his cover, guns raised, ready to take on whoever was firing at his vehicle. There was nothing to shoot at, but Nox went with his gut and hit the trigger anyway.

He heard the grunt of a man, but couldn't tell where the body was. All he saw was that same row of cactus plants ahead of him, and his monowheel laying down in the dirt.

That was when one of the cacti keeled over, and Nox could see that it was no ordinary plant. The insides were hollowed out, and dangling from the opening at the bottom Nox could see the feet of the man inside. No wonder Nox couldn't see their shadows. He wasn't looking for the ones the cacti made.

Chapter Twenty-two

THE CACTUS EYE GANG

"Parley!" came a voice from another cactus just like the last one. It moved, the arms folding in like an accordion. Across the way, another one hopped along the desert towards the fallen gunslinger. It was like something you'd see in a children's play, but this stage was life, and right now the Coilhunter was the director.

When the two other cactus-covered gunners reached their comrade, they pulled down their green hoods to show their sweaty faces beneath. And you thought it was warm in the desert already. Try wearing the desert as an extra layer.

They were the Cactus Eye Gang, a trio of siblings who'd won every sharpshooting contest at every fair throughout the land. There was the oldest, Cactus Candy, and she was a tall, slender woman, built like a rifle, with a mouth to match. Then there was Cactus Cody, the youngest, barely sixteen, but with an easy sixteen kills to his name. And then there was Cactus Casey, the middle child, who they say is often neglected. Well, they'd neglect him a lot more now that he was lying dead in the dirt.

"You killed our brother, you damn rattlesnake!"

Cactus Candy roared, and her lion's mane of sandy hair quivered as she spoke. They all had that same thick mop of dirty blonde, as if God'd given up and just put glue on their crowns and shoved them head-first in the sand.

"If ya heard me rattle," Nox rasped, "then why'd ya shoot?"

"I'll get 'em good," young Cactus Cody volunteered, just like he probably volunteered for everything. He was filled with the enthusiasm of youth. There were a lot of ways to sap you of that, and Nox had six of them in that pistol of his.

"Put down the gun or I'll put it down for ya," Nox warned. "Or I'll put you down too."

"You don't go near 'im!" Cactus Candy bellowed. She aimed a shot at Nox's head, and he could almost feel the crosshairs, like the pinprick of the rays of the sun.

"We've got two choices," Nox said. "We can all walk away from here. Well, you two can. Or we can click empty and see who's left standin'. You might be the best sharpshooters this land has seen, but let me remind you o' somethin': you're shootin' against *me*."

Now, vengeance was a funny thing. It made you do things you ought not to. It made you take risks you couldn't afford to take. Right then and there, Nox could see the vengeance in Cactus Candy's eyes. He knew it, because he saw it in his own eyes when he dared to look in a mirror. He'd gotten his vengeance, sure, but he still avoided the looking glass.

"Think it through," Nox said. "You've got one brother to bury. You wanna make that two?"

"Let me at 'im!" Cactus Cody said, but his sister held him back. You see, family was a funny thing too. It was something that fuelled that vengeance, and it was something that doused the flames. Too many families in the Wild North had let the fire consume them, and they'd lost more to the inferno because of it. Cactus Candy wasn't just sharp with her shooting. She was sharp in her head as well. Well, that was rare.

"Don't give 'im an excuse," Cactus Candy told her brother.

"Not that I need one," Nox said, "but you already gave me plenty."

"We'll give ya plenty more!" Cody shouted. He was old enough to not be a so-called demon, but he was young enough to go to Hell. Nox didn't like it any more than the next bounty hunter, but the gangs started you young. Crime didn't have an age requirement, nor a right of passage. And it sure didn't matter to the victim if it was an old hand or a young one that held the pistol.

"Tell me," Nox said. "Why are you out here?"

"Sunbathin'," Cactus Candy said.

"Oh, ya catch many rays in those suits o' yours?"

"The sun ain't good for ya."

"No, it ain't. But I ain't good for ya either. Now, let me repeat that question, and let me tell ya that I don't like repeatin' things. Why are ya out here?"

"To kill you, o' course."

"Who sent ya?"

"I think you know the answer."

"Maybe I do, but I wanna hear ya say it."

"The Songsnatcher."

"Is he here?"

Cactus Candy laughed. "Why would he bother with you?"

"So, this is just a distraction then."

"Well, we sure distracted ya, huh?"

"Not as much as I distracted your brother there," Nox said, nodding towards the corpse of Cactus Casey. He wondered if he'd cook quicker in that suit of his.

Yet again, Cactus Candy had to hold young Cody back.

"Where is he now?" Nox asked.

"In heaven," Cody said. "But you won't be."

"I mean the Songsnatcher."

"He doesn't tell us that," Cactus Candy explained. "All we know is he's goin' from town to town, clearin' out the little ones."

"And that rests right with ya?"

"About as right as *this* rests with you," she replied, pointing down to Cactus Casey's body. Oh, you could start to smell the stench already, but then maybe that was his living aroma. God help them if they didn't get him to the grave soon.

"Well, you got your distraction," Nox said, "and you got a little extra too. Cut your losses and walk away. You ain't my target, but if you get in my way again, you will be."

"Okay," Cactus Candy said coolly.

"You're just gonna let 'im leave?" Cody asked with incredulity.

"No," Nox said. "She's lettin' you leave without leavin' in a body bag."

Nox backed away, watching them both carefully for any sign of the embers of vengeance. Oh, they were in their eyes still, but so long as they stayed there and didn't go to their gun arms, that was just fine. Nox knew he could take them both now that they were out in the open, and Cactus Candy likely knew that too. Remember, she was a sharp one.

Nox hauled his monowheel up, keeping his gun eyes on the duo until he could pull his pistol back out to do the pointing for him. He checked the tank, which hadn't emptied, and rolled it back to the cactus he'd hid behind before, parking it against the spine-tree.

He strolled back out into the open as the Cactus Eye Gang—if you could call two a gang—watched with withering glares. Then he picked up his guitar and hung it on his back. This time the strings twanged noisily. Nox didn't try to mute them. Just like the percussion of gunfire, the Coilhunter was done hiding more than hunting. The noise told you he was ready. It told you he was coming. He hoped the Songsnatcher was listening, but even if he wasn't, sooner or later, delay or no delay, he'd make him hear.

Chapter Twenty-three

SHOOTOUT AT
THE REGISTRY ROYALE

Due east of Oldtown there was a little establish-ment known as Tylerstown, bordering the site of M.L. Tyler's Ironworks, one of the newer iron mines to sprout up from the sand in recent years. The old gold rush was long over, but the rush for iron was as fresh as ever. Morgan Longtooth Tyler knew that better than most. That's why he had the slag heaps "mined" in a different way, as far too many would-be iron thieves found out.

But Tylerstown wasn't just a mining colony. It was known for Morgan's other pastimes, which included mapmaking and genealogy. Why, he even ran a little registry office, which he dubbed the Registry Royale. Folk from all over the Wild North, and even some down south, made the pilgrimage to find out what he knew about their families, or to sell him papers and documents for a handful of iron.

Morgan Tyler didn't put mines around the Reg-istry Royale, but he did employ a two dozen strong guard, armed to the teeth—and trained to bite. It was lucky he did, because on that morning, as he was having his coffee over an old map of Altadas before the Iron Empire came, the Songsnatcher showed up.

They saw him coming in a haze on the horizon, first on horseback and then on foot as he got closer. He was suited up against the sun, but maybe more against the bullets. There weren't many like him in those parts, and few who'd dare take on the Registry Royale alone.

He started with a rifle, falling to one knee to take aim. He took out the first guard standing outside the building, blasting in the window for good measure. Then he took out the next two as they ran out the door to greet him. Why, he would've been content if they'd just waved at him from afar. Again the guards came, and again the Songsnatcher gunned them down. Hell, they just ran into the bullets.

Then the Songsnatcher cast aside his rifle as he marched on up to the blasted doors. He kicked through the splinters and advanced through the building, slow and steady, then quick as lightning as he unleashed two singlesticks to batter the legs and arms of the remaining guards inside. He beat them black and blue, or bloodied them red. He caved in their skulls and cracked their bones. He left them as dead as he left the bullet-ridden guards outside, except he made a spectacle of it. The maps lining the walls had plenty of new red ink.

"Whoever paid you, I'll pay double," Morgan Tyler said. He held both his hands up before him, but couldn't hold the shake.

"I'm not here for a sourdough like you," the Songsnatcher said, but that wasn't much relief. "I'm here for your papers."

"M-my papers?"

"You have the largest registry of people in this land. Names. Locations. Dates. I want you to comb your records, and comb 'em quick. I want you to find the name and location of every child born after the Harvest."

"B-but why?"

"If you're askin' that, then you haven't heard o' me yet, and that's probably a good thing. Let's hope, for your sake, you don't have any young children too."

Chapter Twenty-four

A PENNY FOR YOUR KILLS

Nox rolled on, slowly now, as his monowheel chugged and spluttered, and one of the metal treads clattered noisily from its loosened casing. That diesel tank had been bandaged up like a head wound, so you couldn't really fault it for nearly giving up the ghost. If you took a bullet to the head, you'd give it up quicker.

He headed back out of tribal territory, abandoning the somewhat greenish fields for the very red ones. It was strange to consider the sand as *comforting*, but the strange reality of humanity was that even the bad things, when you were exposed to them often enough, became their own form of comfort. Sometimes folk were more afraid to embrace the good, the new, the unknown. The caged bird. Or, well, the devil you know. You had to wonder if there even had to be a devil. Yet, in the Wild North, you knew there was more than one, and you might've known them both.

He spotted white-haired Five-pence Tully in the Mounds not far from Oldtown. The Mounds were semi-permanent sand dunes, built from a layer of sand blown over an old mountain range. They were the perfect place for the wildlife to retreat to, and for the criminals to set up camp, and for that wandering photographer-for-hire to get some good pictures. Usually pictures of the bad.

When Nox made his way up to her vantage point, he found her facing off against a bandit, who was looking to steal all that valuable equipment of hers. Now, you'd think the Coilhunter might've got involved in that. After all, he didn't need a Wanted poster when he was witness to the crime. But he sat back in his seat, placed his hands behind his head, and put his feet up on the steering wheel. It was nice to have the day off.

"I'll shoot, I swear!" the bandit told Tully, who simply stood there, hand on hip, waiting patiently for him to honour his word.

"Let me shoot ya first," she replied, and she buried her head back unto the blanket of her dark chamber— known by some simply as a *camera*. Others just called it magic.

"Say *please*," she told the bandit, who stood a little dumbfounded in front of the lens.

And then, with a click of the shutter, a bullet fired from the camera and took that bandit out cold. It also took a photograph of the kill. You see, Five-pence Tully sold those for a pretty penny. You could've said she made a killing twice.

"Good shot," Nox said, as he strolled on over.

Tully shoved a handful of her wild hair up over her head and fanned the photograph by her face. It was mighty warm out. "It is, ain't it?" She showed the moment of surprise, caught in black and white, and a little bit of red, on that bandit's face. Oh, she'd earn plenty for that one.

"Got anything for me?" Nox asked her.

She kicked at a rucksack by her supplies. Nox bent down and went through the contents, which had dozens of photographs, all shapes and sizes. Some of them were of those on Nox's Wanted list. There was even a photo of Sam Silver and Dozen-gun Dan, looking all too friendly. But it was the pictures of the Songsnatcher he was after. And boy did she have some.

"Where's the last spottin'?" he asked.

"Not far from here," she said, before slurping down some beans straight from the can. She patted her bulbous belly, as if to help the beans go down. "He was up by Tylerstown, then passed through Oldtown on the way back." She took another swig of beans and spoke the next bit with her mouth full. "Took half the kids with 'im."

"So he did," Nox said, as he found photographic evidence of the crime. It showed the Songsnatcher using what at first glance looked like a tribal blowdart, but might've actually been a flute. It wasn't clear why none of the townsfolk went to the aid of their kids.

"And he just waltzed on through?"

"Well, he didn't quite waltz," Tully said. "Wasn't playin' the right music for it. It was lucky I had earmuffs on or I might've dozed off too. Looked like the children were sleepwalkin' more than anything."

"And you didn't try and stop 'im?"

"That's not our arrangement." She offered the can of beans to Nox, but he shook his head. "Besides, I thought you didn't let anyone take your kills?"

"I don't. But I'll let you take the photographs. What do I owe ya?"

"It's more than the usual for this lot."

Nox felt the weight of the rucksack again. "It sure is."

"Make it three usuals and we'll call it even steven."

Nox opened a pouch on his belt and thumbed fifteen coils into his hand.

"Three usuals," he said, as he handed them to her. "And the body for free, I imagine."

"Well, ain't you one with a big imagination. Yeah, you can take 'im. Might be a bounty on 'im all the same. Sands, you might be makin' back those there coils for my here kill."

"All part of the arrangement," Nox replied, and you could've almost seen the hint of a smile in his eyes. Just a hint though, enough to leave you guessing. But if it was anger in those peepers, and you were the criminal staring into them, you didn't have to guess at all.

"How are ya gonna get 'im back?" Tully asked. She reefed a chunk of bread with her teeth and offered it again to Nox. He refused, but he was starting to feel hungry. He instinctively pawed at his ration pouch on his belt. "That wheel of yours looks like it's keelin' over," Tully continued. "Don't tell me ya had that tinker friend o' yours patchin' it up."

"I won't tell ya then," Nox replied. "But don't you worry your white hair about the body. You leave that to me."

"Oh, I'm leavin' it."

Nox rummaged through the pockets of the dead bandit, taking a few of his supplies, and two quarter coils for good measure. You'd think Tully would've done that, but she made plenty from her photographs. Hell, she made twice as much by selling pictures of the criminals to Nox, and pictures of Nox to the criminals. The Coilhunter knew well about her double-dealing, but at least she was dealing in the first place. She only killed if she was attacked.

Nox dragged the body to the edge of the slope, hammered a few buttons on his monowheel, and then sat back in the seat to wait. He was tempted to have those rations now, but he knew that Five-pence Tully was just gunning to get a picture of him with his mask off. He tolerated her, but he wasn't going to indulge her, that's for sure.

After half an hour, where Tully loitered more than she needed, pretending to take photographs of the sand and the sun, a bird appeared in the sky, and then another, and several more behind. They looked like a passing flock at first, until they started to draw near. That's when you could make out the glint of the sun off their metal pieces. No, those were no creatures of nature. They were creatures of Nox.

The mechanical carrion birds flapped in and circled overhead just like the real thing, ready to pounce on the corpse below. But they weren't there to devour the flesh. They were there to lift it up and carry it away. Their claws were grapnel hooks, and they dug deep into the bandit's clothes and skin. It took all eight of them to lift the body, and it looked like at any moment they might drop him. Not that it mattered. He couldn't get any more dead.

Then Nox heard a loud click and saw a bright flash from Tully's camera. He eyed her up there on the higher hill and shook his head.

"What?" she shouted down to him. "Consider it a tip!"

Chapter Twenty-five

THE MASSACRE OF MUSIC

The Coilhunter's next destination was the Song-snatcher's last: Oldtown. He found that settlement up in arms after that last attack, once the folk had woken up from the Songsnatcher's forced slumber. They might not have known who was behind it if it weren't for Deaf Debby, who hadn't heard the music at all.

Nox expected an uproar, but what he found was a mob. The townsfolk had the local band strung up and were hurling abuse at the bodies. It was bad enough to die by the neck, but something else to have folk throwing rotten food at your corpse. Then again, if they were going to do that, maybe it was better to be dead.

Nox watched as another gang dragged a man from his house. A few stragglers brought out his musical instruments. One of them bashed the violin over the man's head.

"Monster!" the people shouted.

"Snatcher!" they cried.

It didn't seem to matter what the man said, what defence or denial he had, nor the fact that not all of those musicians could be the Songsnatcher. The anger had taken them, and just like those embers in Cactus Candy's eyes, Nox saw them burning bright in the eyes of everyone present. The only eyes they didn't burn in were the eyes of those hanging by the rope.

That wasn't a good day to carry a musical instrument. And that was when they spotted Nox, the Coilhunter, with that good old guitar of his strapped to his back. You should've seen their eyes then.

Chapter Twenty-six

THAT GOOD OL' GUITAR

"Coilhunter!" one of them shouted.

"It's the Coilhunter!" another added.

"It's him!" came a third.

Then the flurry of voices grew louder and angrier, and it was harder to tell what they said. It might've been "Get 'im!" It might've been "He killed 'em!" It might've been "Murderer!" It might've even been "Songsnatcher!"

They came like the village folk with pitchforks of old, but this time they came with wooden bats and bayonets. They crowded around him, row after row, pushing and shoving, flowing back and forth like a tidal wave of rage.

He tried to explain himself. He tried to deny their accusations. He tried to make them see that he wasn't the villain, that he was hunting the Songsnatcher just like them. But all they saw was a masked figure with his guitar strapped to his back. All they saw was a snatcher and his song.

The noise was deafening. No one could hear his word. The shoves became rougher now. He was barely pushed an inch before someone on the other side pushed back more violently. Then the punches came. Soon, it'd be the weapons.

Nox knew he couldn't reason with them. He couldn't fight them either, and couldn't kill them. They were not the bad guys. They were the folk who'd been far too often wronged. He could've sent some of them to sleep with his butterflies, but that would've only added to the illusion that he was in the wrong. Besides, he didn't have enough capsules for the lot of them. No, this would require something else.

This would require a rocket.

The Coilhunter's newly-added jet propulsion system was crude, and Nox wasn't even sure if it'd work in the heat of battle. He grasped two ring pulls on either side of his oxygen tank, where the rocket was attached, and pulled the cords up tight. A blast of fuel ignited in the rocket, sending out a thick billowing cloud of smoke. Nox sent his own from his mask for good measure as some in the crowd froze or backed away.

Then, after what seemed like several seconds where the rocket wouldn't fire, it suddenly blasted skyward, taking the Coilhunter with it, and one or two townsfolk, who fell back into the maddened—and now confused and awed—crowd.

Chapter Twenty-seven

HARD LANDING

Nox soared through the sky and hurtled across the landscape. He shook violently with the rattle of the rocket. He had to squint his eyes against the breeze and the dust. If he wasn't wearing a mask, the force of the wind would've sent his cheeks flapping.

He watched as the world below him fell away, as the dunes turned to grains and the people turned to ants. He'd once seen the world like this before, but that time he was *in* the rocket, not strapped to it. Unlike most of his gadgets, this wasn't one he could control. It got him up and away, but that was it. Yet that was everything in that moment. Sometimes you only need a hammer for a nail. And sometimes you need a rocket for a getaway.

Nox tried to see where the propulsion device was taking him. Up and away was one thing, but that could bring him anywhere. If he were a betting man, he would've bet on landing somewhere in the sun-coloured sands. He would've gambled on red.

But the violence of the rocket, of the fuel blast, of the rushing wind, tore at his face and his features, and at the rocket and oxygen tank on his back. The straps attached to his shoulders dug in deep, and yet even with the thunder of the rocket and the sharp whistle of the wind, he could hear the tearing of one of those straps.

He grasped at it instinctively, just like reaching for his gun, and caught the fabric just in time before it flailed away. He pulled it close, tensing every muscle in his body to hold it down as the wind tugged back on it with an even tighter grip.

He was still a hundred feet in the air and had no way to jettison the rocket so he could float on down with his driftwings. He was entirely at the mercy of the fuel-guzzling, wind-roaring beast that'd launched him into the heavens, a machine some would call a godseeker. But there was only one real way to seek God in the Wild North. You didn't look for him a hundred feet above. You looked for him six feet below.

And that was where the rocket sent him. It reached the fullness of its ascent, then turned, and then started back towards land when the fires spluttered out. There was no coal to feed it. There was no engine to crank. There was now just a hunk of metal attached to a man, and a strap getting looser by the second.

It fell, and the Coilhunter fell. And Nox knew from the fastness of the descent that it was going to be a hard landing. He tried to get his wings out to help the fall, but in the process he lost his grip on the strap and found himself yanked out of his backpack altogether. The wind ripped off his mask and sent his oxygen tank somersaulting down a nearby dune. And it sent the Coilhunter tumbling down another.

Chapter Twenty-eight

CAUGHT BETWEEN
THE DEVIL AND THE DUST

The first gasp was always the worst. The air stung like a thousand needles, stabbing his lungs simultaneously as he breathed in, so much so that he didn't want to expand them any further. He exhaled just as quickly, and that hurt less, but he needed to get the air in, get the oxygen in. His air tank, with all its pain-numbing chemicals, was gone. He hadn't seen where it landed in the flurry of his fall.

He tried to clamber up, exposing his scarred face to the indignity of the sun, but his lungs felt as though they were being crushed. How quick it was, this turnaround from a man who could master most, who could leap up buildings and draw in darkness, to a man who could barely walk, now barely stumble, now barely crawl.

When faced with a moment like that, all you wanted to do was lie there and rest, but your lungs wouldn't let you. They begged for good, clean, filtered, chemically-enhanced air. And if they didn't get it, then you could lie there and rest forever more.

He pulled a small mouthpiece from his belt, which had a tiny vat of oxygen attached, just enough for a few puffs of air. He breathed in until it clicked empty, like a pistol without another round. One to give life, one to take it. Why, you could say God was somewhere there doing the same, making his own gadgets and guns.

He found the rocket that'd been his momentary escape from doom, and now his doomer, crashed and crinkled, sending up a plume of dark smoke like a beacon. Oh, it would doom him anew if it could lure the strange beasts of the wild to him, or alert the ruffians and the robbers and the scavengers to his whereabouts.

It was a one-use rocket. Nox knew that for the most part, but he largely only knew it in theory before. Now he knew it like you knew something else that was pretty fundamental: it was a one-use life you got there. Better use it wisely. Better not attach it to a rocket.

He continued on, one aching limb in front of the other, one aching lungful of air to make them move. If that old house fire that had got his family and then got his face had stopped there, it wouldn't have been so bad. But the smoke got him deeper and left him with scars within. And you didn't speak of the figurative ones. Those were the ones for other folk to make stories about. The Man with the Unseen Scars.

He reached the top of one dune and tried to stand up, but collapsed just as quickly. He thought he caught a glimpse of something glinting from the sunlight on another dune far ahead, but he couldn't get a good enough look before he tumbled head over heels down his current sand mound. It didn't look good, and didn't feel good, but at least it got him closer to that metal object.

He gasped and wheezed. He sounded more and more like an old man, getting closer and closer to his final breaths. He knew if he couldn't find his oxygen tank soon, he was done for. He wouldn't die immediately. No, he'd lose consciousness first. Then maybe he'd see his life flash before his eyes, and see a thousand flashes for each of his names. And maybe he'd see the faces of his loved ones, of his dead wife and dead kids. And maybe he'd see the faces of the ones he'd hunted, of those dead gangsters and dead killers. And maybe he wouldn't know which he'd smile at more.

He reached the glinting object, but it wasn't the oxygen tank he sought. It was his steel-plated guitar, which had partially gotten him into this mess. The land was strewn with reminders of his shortcomings. In a moment like that, he felt like there might be a million more of them, one for each and every grain.

And yet, just as his lungs felt like they were collapsing, just as the world seemed to darken, he spotted another glinting object not far off. It was just metres away, and even with his eyes glazing over he could see the shape of the oxygen vat, half-buried in the sand. He knew he had to get to it quick or when the sandstorms came, it wouldn't just bury the other half. It'd bury him.

He summoned what little strength he had left— what little life he had too—and scrambled over on his elbows to the prized object. He seized it and pulled one of the severed pipes up and shoved it into his mouth. He inhaled as hard as he could, sucking in the oxygen and the chemical mixture, which worked in seconds to bring him back from the brink.

He collapsed there for a moment, suckling on the tube like a baby on the teat, just as much a life-giving moment, nursing himself back to the gunslinging, scum-hunting Man with a Thousand Names. The sun shifted past its peak, passing on in disgust when it could no longer stare down at his dying form, and Nox finally sat up and fixed the oxygen tank and mask back into their proper place. He patched up the strap, like the thread of life tied anew, and got up onto his now steady feet, ready to see what part of the land he'd actually landed in.

In the grim, sun-scorched wastes of the Wild North, the dust was everywhere. It was your bed and your bedfellow. It was your cradle and your grave. Try all you might, you couldn't escape it. Folk said even if you tried, it'd just find you again, like a bounty hunter. They said sometimes you didn't have a choice. Sometimes you were caught between the Devil and the dust. Nox glanced up to see what was making that whirling sound in the distance, and saw the spinning dust devils approaching fast. Yeah, and sometimes you got them both in one.

Chapter Twenty-nine

DUST COUNTRY

This was Dust Country, one of the many cousin territories of the Devil's March down south, regions that belonged to no one but the dust and the wind, and those freaks of nature they sent spinning through the sand. You couldn't live there. You couldn't mine there. A few unwise folk had tried, and there were a few signs and flags declaring ownership buried beneath the dunes. The bodies? Well, who knows where they were.

Nox knew one thing: he could've gotten out of there quick if he'd had his monowheel, though even then he knew it wouldn't be easy. But on foot was different. On foot was deadly. That damn rocket'd gotten him out of one trap and sent him into another. Some folk spoke about frying pans and fires. They never spoke about the wind.

The dust devils were far off for now, little tornadoes of sand, some hovering in one spot, others leisurely roaming, and others still darting around in a frenzy, as if there wasn't enough sand to consume. Well, there were always the bones of men. Men like the Coilhunter.

Nox took out his eyeglass and scanned the area.

He wasn't entirely familiar with this land, because folk didn't go here—for good reason. This was one of nature's last enclaves, and it grew a little every year as the workings of the weather pushed the sandbanks out further. There was only one God, but there was always room for more devils.

There was no noticeable exit, and the landscape looked similar in all directions, with the dust devils spread out relatively equally. Chance had put him bang smack in the middle of Dust Country, and chance wasn't betting on him making it out alive. If you were going to trust in the spinning table, you'd trust the spinning sand even more.

Nox knew he couldn't loiter there to plan things out. The sun was getting lower, and night wasn't much more merciful. At least day showed where those dust devils roamed. The last thing he needed was to wander that landscape blind.

He headed south-east, trusting that at least that would get him closer to familiar territory, to a semblance of civilisation—and one that wasn't out to kill him. Well, one that didn't have him top of the list. He limped, still exhausted from his prior struggle. His oxygen tank had lost some of its supply and was buckled badly, just like his bruised guitar, but at least he could breathe again. The pain-numbing cocktail was kicking in, but he could still feel the pressure in his lungs. The pain was gone, but the pressure would stay for a day or two. And maybe life would stay a little longer.

The dust devils were far-off initially, but the fast ones, which folk dubbed whirler-dashers, travelled quicker than he limped. The slow ones, the steady-swirlers, could be mostly avoided. But the sand was a father and the wind a mother, and they could birth new dust devils all the time. Some collapsed here, and others formed there, and everywhere the landscape shifted and changed with them, twirling up or falling down into another new dune.

Nox picked up the pace, but even as he did, so did one of the whirler-dashers to his left. It raced towards him, and as he ran he wasn't sure if he should keep going, stop, turn back, or take a different direction altogether. But there was no time to think or assess. All he had was his instincts and his trained legs, trained more for the hunt than the flight, but boy did he flee. He narrowly charged out of the way of that passing dust devil, which was big enough to pick him up and batter him and spit him out like yet another grain of sand.

He halted suddenly as a steady-swirler spun up from nothing before him and hovered there on the spot, blocking his path ahead. He glanced back and shielded his eyes from the darting devil behind him, which zig-zagged around his back to peg him in. You'd almost swear they were sentient, and the tribesfolk claimed they were. Some of them said they were the spirits of ancestors. Others said they were fairy winds. Others still said they were trapped demons, which would've rather been trapped inside the bodies of men.

The hovering whirlwind ahead died suddenly and Nox darted forward through its remains. He continued on, picking up speed as he saw several dust devils draw in together on a collision course to his right. The largest of them swallowed the others, bulging out into a bigger beast of nature with the power to kill as much as toss and throw. It made for the Coilhunter now, intent on swallowing him as well.

Nox ran from it, then turned sharply as another whirler-dasher crossed his path, then turned back as a new one rose there, then turned again as he stumbled upon a steady-swirler. The path ahead was a maze of dust devils, but not a maze you could map, with the sand-hedges changing by the second. And you didn't want to get to the centre. You wanted to get out.

A clearing opened up ahead of him and he made a dash for it. Then suddenly another birthed anew right beneath his feet as he ran. It sucked him up and spun him in the air. If he wasn't wearing that mask, and didn't have that oxygen tank strapped to his back, the very air might've been sucked out of his lungs. The world spun around him, making him nauseous, and the sand tore at his face, stinging the cuts and bruises.

Then the dust devil died just as suddenly, and he fell from a great height, high enough to break bones and crush skulls. Even though his head still swam, he had just enough concentration, and that greater store of muscle memory and instinct, to open his drifter wings. The wooden and steel-plated panels caught the wind and he sailed onwards. It took him a moment to realise he was sailing back towards the centre of Dust Country, but not a moment more to turn back south-east.

He glided on, dropping altitude, but now turning

this way and that as more dust devils came into his path. A few small ones weren't tall enough to reach him, and a few others could reach, but weren't powerful enough to do much more than shake him as he flew. Yet others were tall and wide, and whirled with an audible rage. You didn't have to be one of the tribesfolk to believe there was a demon in them then.

The whirl of one clipped his left wing and almost pulled him in. He dipped lower, then turned sideways as another burst from the ground. Then he zig-zagged through a row of steady sand columns, and turned sharply out of the way of another whirler-dasher as his feet grazed the ground. He folded up his wings just in time to avoid one last dust devil ahead before he clambered up the tall barrier dune and slid down the other side.

Finally, Nox emerged from Dust Country, tired but alive, if only temporarily. You see, the whole of the Wild North was its own Dust Country, and there were devils that stayed still and devils that ran quick—and those devils were called men.

Chapter Thirty

A MEETIN' OF MARRED MINDS

In an undisclosed location in the Wild North, as empty of features as most other locations—and thus difficult to find and difficult to track—the Songsnatcher hosted a meeting with his growing group of followers, those who bought into the story that there were demons out there, inhabiting the bodies of their children. It was a wild story, some might've even said a crazy one, but after everything the people of the world of Altadas had experienced over the past fifteen years, it was a believable story all the same.

"The Coilhunter is on to us," the Songsnatcher declared. "We've delayed him as much as possible, but now he's closin' in. That means we need to up the ante. That means we need to speed up the process of extraction and elimination. If we don't, we lose this fleetin' opportunity, and the Coilhunter will stop our noble pursuit."

There weren't cheers, but there might've been if the mood wasn't quite so sombre. Instead, there were nods. Lots of nods from lots of heads from lots of folk who'd lost kids to the Iron Empire. It was easy to see why they'd become jaded to the world, even after the Iron Empire fell. You could defeat evil, but you couldn't fully remove its stains. And folk said that sometimes, if you scrubbed them too much, you could expose the evil inside you too.

"We'll root 'em out," Devilbane Higgins said, a clean-shaven, piercing-eyed, hiss-tongued gentleman, with all the gentleness of a sledgehammer. And he carried one too. He was the leader of the growing militia amassed in support of the Songsnatcher's plan. He was a religious type, with a God-given mission, and some said the Songsnatcher played him like a violin. He was a musician after all.

The surviving Cactus Eye Gang arrived by motorcycle late to the meeting. They'd barely stopped their vehicles before hopping off and marching in, pushing through the crowd.

"You're late," the Songsnatcher stated.

"We were held up, holdin' up the Coilhunter," young Cody explained.

"Hard to find ya out here too," Cactus Candy said.

"Good," the Songsnatcher replied. "It means he'll have a harder time too." He paused. "Why are there only two o' ya?"

Cactus Candy sunk her head. "He got Casey."

"Dead?"

"Dead as that Coilhunter'll be!" Cody roared.

"Use that anger. We'll need it. But for now, save it and store it until the next time you see 'im. And don't let 'em make you a gang o' one, or a gang o' none."

He turned sharply, letting his coat flail just like the Coilhunter's did. It was small wonder that folk thought it was him. He unfurled a giant map of the

Wild North and held it down on the sand with tribal tokens. It looked like he'd collected quite a few, and they weren't all from the same tribe.

"This is where I need you to be," the Songsnatcher said, pointing to the southern town of Bellford. "The records show a high number of children there, on account o' the school. Some send their children there from other towns too. Time it right and you can take 'em all."

"And where'll you be?" Cactus Candy asked.

"I'll be pickin' up another weapon. I'll be gettin' a child close to the Coilhunter's heart."

Chapter Thirty-one

THAT SONG OF SLUMBER

In the central north of the Wild North, just outside of the tribal territory of the peace-loving Ootana, Handcart Ranch was its own peaceful abode. It wasn't always like that, and its owner, Sally Hays—or Handcart Sally as she was better known—had a way of attracting attention to herself just like the Coilhunter, and sometimes because of him. But now was a quiet time, a time for working the land and tending the horses, and raising those two kids who weren't hers, and yet came to be hers all the same.

Laura was sixteen, and Luke was eleven and one month. He claimed he was a man now, but he still did what kids did and counted the months. The grown-ups of the Wild North might've been wise to do the same, because many couldn't afford to count the years. You just didn't get enough of them. So, you could put twenty years on that gravestone of yours, or you could put two hundred and forty months. Hell, maybe you should count in days instead.

"He's doin' it again," Laura shouted out to Sally, who was hauling haystacks into the paddock. Most of the horses were new, and most of them were the Ootana sort that spooked easy, but they settled in quick and seemed like they were there to last. Of course, Sally had thought that about the previous lot, before the deadwalkers came.

"He's doin' what?" Sally called back.

Laura folded her arms over her plaid shirt. "Bein' weird."

"I ain't bein' weird," Luke said, as he nudged past Laura, pushing her into the door frame. She shoved him back for good measure.

"You are too. First it was you sleepin' with your rifle like a teddy bear. Then it was you patrollin' the ranch like you was a sheriff. Now it's you drawin' nothin' but Wanted posters in that sketchbook o' yours."

"So what? I ain't allowed to draw now?"

"If it's to impress Nox, it won't do it, ya know."

"It ain't to impress him," Luke replied, and he couldn't pout any more. "Why'd I wanna impress him? He ain't nobody to us."

"He is too. He's—"

"Don't you say it! He ain't our papa. And *she*," Luke said, pointing a shaking finger at Sally across the way, "ain't our momma."

"She's more a momma to us than ours ever was."

Luke's voice grew weaker. "I don't wanna think 'bout that."

"You have to, Luke," Laura said, as she put a hand on her brother's shoulder. "You have to get it out. I thought that was what the drawin' was for."

Luke shrugged off her embrace. "It's nothin' but pictures, Laura. It don't mean nothin'."

"What're you two fightin' 'bout now?" Sally asked,

as she drew up. She took off her gloves and hung them on her belt, then used her chequered sleeves to wipe the sweat and dirt from her brow. She fanned her face with her straw hat.

"Him bein' weird again," Laura said.

"I ain't bein' weird!" Luke shouted.

"You're bein' weird right now."

"Cut it out, you two. Laura, stop pesterin' your brother. Luke … go out an' groom your horse, will ya?"

"She's not my horse," Luke said, and his temper faded, and his voice grew dispassionate. "I killed my horse. Remember?"

Sally could remember, though she wasn't there to witness it. The Coilhunter had told her about it. Luke had caved that horse's head in with a rock. He said it was because of the deadwalkers, but the way Nox looked at her, she knew it was something else, something more. If it was just the deadwalkers, he could've used a gun. It was a funny old world when you thought someone not using a gun was maybe more dangerous.

"She's gettin' lonely out there," Sally told the boy. "You not ever gonna ride her?"

"She's not my horse," Luke said again, and he walked back inside and went upstairs.

Laura raised her eyebrows. "Told you he's bein' weird."

"Go set the table," Sally replied. "I want an early night tonight."

They had supper, and only Sally and Laura talked. Luke ate with one hand and drew another Wanted poster with the other. They were all of fictional villains, some just like those the Coilhunter faced, and others like something out of a nightmare. Every so often he drew the Coilhunter too, and he looked like both.

They retired to bed, and the ranch seemed quiet and peaceful. Maybe it was because of the hard day's work that tired their joints and muscles. Maybe it was because of the summer breeze that wafted in the slightly open windows. Or maybe it was because of that calming music, which sent them off into a deeper slumber, dreaming of good things, of pleasant things. They didn't dream of the Songsnatcher playing his flute outside. They didn't dream of the haunting music that made Luke stir in his sleep. They didn't dream of the boy getting up and walking through the house. They didn't dream of him opening that front door and leaving it ajar as he walked straight towards a parked half-tread truck outside. They didn't dream of him opening the door at the back of the truck and climbing into the cages inside, where dozens more children were crowded, cold and cramped, scared and shivering. No, they didn't dream of that at all.

Chapter Thirty-two

ZONE RESONANCE

Most outposts in the Wild North were what you'd call "quiet towns," with just a few houses, a local shop, and, of course, a place to drown your desert sorrows. Well, Bellford wasn't one of them. Not only did it not have a saloon—a successful effort by the puritans in charge—but it was big and sprawling and loud in comparison to the other civilised places. And that was mostly down to the few hundred children who either lived and learned there, or were brought in from other towns on both sides of the border. You see, Bellford was all about its children and their education. It used to belong on the border itself, and that was the *ford* in its name, until the borders changed in the war, and it had the biggest bell-tower in the wastes, attached to that big cloistered school in the centre. Why, it was a veritable miracle it stood in that lawless land at all.

You see, Bellford was noisy, but it was peaceful too. The puritan leadership outlawed weapons, and Bellford was mostly left alone by the bandits and the gangs. For those who dared defy its laws, there was a local marshal, Eleanor "No-gun" Pickett, who kept the peace, and, as you could guess from the name, she did it with just her bare hands. She wasn't alone though. Her posse, the No-gun Marshals, trained three times a week in a martial art called *askarochi*, or "round hand," which was taught by the Nusodee tribe.

Bellford, therefore, wasn't going to be an easy target for the Cactus Eye Gang and the Songsnatcher's militia. But it was a target all the same.

It was a school day when the attack came, and it came in the morning, while many of the children were still on their way. Several dozen tykes roamed the desert on their own, carrying bags on their little backs or in their little hands, loaded with books that were outlawed in Iron Empire territory. Those were the first children to be snatched.

The half-tread trucks blazed in, their engines roaring, their wheels and tracks tearing through the sand and kicking up dust in their wake. Immediately, the children ran. Some cast aside their books, while others cradled them to their chest, their few possessions in a land that encouraged—even required—much darker and deadlier ones.

The militia hung from the side of the trucks, from the doors and windows, from the handholds and nettings, and grabbed the children as they trundled past. They weren't the fastest vehicles in the land, but they didn't have to be. They were faster than all those little legs.

The screams were deafening, but they were muted by the rumble of machinery and now by the school bell, which rang to announce the start of the school day. These children were late, but it wouldn't matter.

The ones inside the school would be next. And they could all be early in Heaven.

A girl tripped ahead of one of the trucks, and she turned and screamed in horror as the vehicle rolled right over her, until the cry cut short, and the truck rocked unsteadily, and the men and women inside tried not to look behind at her body pressed into the sand. All they hoped was that the girl was demon spawn, which by her age they assumed she was, and then they could sleep soundly again. If not, the Songsnatcher could send them to the world of restful slumber.

The trucks rolled into Bellford faster than the townsfolk had time to react. Some mothers grabbed their children before they could be grabbed by the militia. Others ran for help. Others threw themselves in front of the vehicles to slow them down. Others were gunned down by the Cactus Eye Gang.

Eleanor "No-gun" Pickett, dressed in a ruffled white shirt and red plaid skirt, with her hair tied up in a neat brown bun, came out of the school just as the first bullets fired. She ran back inside and called out to Helen "All-arms" Clanton and June "Four-fist" Fisher, her two deputy marshals who worked as part-time teachers. The trio rolled up their sleeves and went outside.

The trucks were already overflowing with children, taken at gunpoint and knifepoint, or just taken by the giant hands of the men and women who snatched them up like little fishes from a lake. They were seized by the collar, crushed in bear hugs, pulled by the ankle, or grabbed by the throat. Not a single child there, no matter how young, was shown any care or mercy, any compassion or empathy. After all, no demons were shown those things either.

Eleanor ducked behind a row of parked half-treads, gesturing for Helen and June to split up in either direction and call in the others. She found one of the trucks unguarded and broke the lock on the back, letting out a flood of captured children, some of whom were caught again almost immediately after. The militia who did the catching were in for a surprise. Eleanor's signature move was a strike to the chest with the edge of her palm, then a poke to the throat with two fingers, and a takedown with a reverse swinging kick. To some, it mirrored the blast of a bullet to the heart, the gurgling of blood in the throat, and the final toppling as the body went down dead. No-gun might've been her nickname, but that didn't mean she didn't hit like one.

The militiaman cried out and lost his weapon with the first strike, and couldn't cry when his vocal box almost caved in from the force of Eleanor's blow. And boy did he fall, for he was a giant of a man, but he had no balance to begin with, and less still after Eleanor's initial hits. She helped a nearby boy to his feet before helping another man off his. Again and again she toppled men and women, some with rifles and some with pistols, but all of them disarmed by the end of it, and all of them dislegged as well.

Across the way to the right, Helen "All-arms" Clanton, slight in form, young and fair, with red hair in pigtails and boots up to her hips, used her own signature move of a flurry of attacks to the face. She hit you on both ears, in both eyes, in the nose and the throat, up the side of your cheek, down the edge of your skull. You didn't know where the attacks were coming from, but you knew for certain they were doing a little bit of brain damage. And then you didn't know much at all.

On the other side, June "Four-fist" Fisher, a black-maned strapper of a woman who some said had eaten her twin in the womb, bowled men over with her bulky shoulders or knocked them out cold with a single well-aimed uppercut to the chin. She was slower than the others, sure enough, but she hit as hard as those half-tread trucks, and that was surer still.

Others of the No-gun Marshals, just shy of a dozen in number, emerged onto the streets of Bellford, and while they were not as well-trained, they fought with everything they had: their hands and feet, their knuckles and their knees. You could run out of ammunition, but not if they were part of you.

The battle raged on the streets, down every alley, even into the homes themselves, where parents fought with fists of their own. Then the townsfolk were pushed back into the school, where tables were turned up for cover, where the children crouched and cowered and covered their heads as the windows blasted apart into a hail of glass shards.

Then the fire came, and that school, a symbol of what the Wild North could ultimately become, blazed like a beacon, or like every campfire around which the gangs and killers warmed their blood-stained hands. The adults and children were smoked out, and the battle raged again on the streets, until eventually the No-gun Marshals were forced to surrender.

They'd fought valiantly, taking down many more militia than their own numbers. But they were still far outnumbered and far outgunned, and they'd lost too many of their own to those outlawed weapons. You see, you could fight a man with fists, but you couldn't fight gunfire. In the end, they were all rounded up, either tied and hoodwinked, or tied and muffled and made to watch as the children they tried to protect were marched onto the trucks.

"You desert hens thought you had us," Devilbane Higgins boasted, "but we're still above snakes, so we are. And maybe we'll feed ya to some!"

"Get a wiggle on, Devilbane," Cactus Candy urged, as she polished her rifle after taking out several Marshals from a distance. "Let's not hang fire any longer than we have to. The master's waitin' for these here shavers back at the ranch."

"I'll dally if God wants me to dally," Devilbane Higgins said. "I ain't here to do the Songsnatcher's work. I'm here for him above and him alone, so I am."

And that might've been true, but some folk said that you could dally in the grave, and some folk said that God had dallied there too.

They loaded up those trucks until they were bursting, until they chugged along even more slowly than they'd come in. But it didn't matter. They'd gotten their catch. And they'd gotten their kills. As far as they were concerned, they'd won this battle, and soon enough they'd win the war against the demon spawn. There was no one out there to slow them and no one out there to stop them.

And so they rolled out, all laughs and smiles to mirror the cries and frowns of the children inside, eyes on the desert tracks behind, eyes on the worn roads ahead. And they didn't see the little mechanical mouse in the sand, watching them from the distance, hinting of another catch—hinting of another kill.

Chapter Thirty-three

A TERRIBLE WAKIN'

Sally Hays screamed when she found the empty room and the empty bed, and the doors wide open. She cried out for Laura, who charged in, still half-asleep, and then raced outside calling her brother's name.

"Luke! Luke! It's not funny, Luke. Come back! Luke!"

But little Luke, once Gun-shy Luke, then Gun-high Luke, and now just another little boy snatched from his cradle, didn't come back. It wasn't funny alright. No one, not even the Songsnatcher himself, was laughing. For him, his aims, his goals, were deadly serious.

Sally Hays came out with her riding gear, and Laura's too, which she dumped on the porch as she kept on walking. There was no time for pleasantries. No time for delays. No time for anything.

"He didn't take his horse," Laura pointed out, as she jogged after her. "What does that mean?"

"I don't know what it means," Sally said. "Let's … let's just find 'im."

They mounted up and rode out, circling the ranch in ever-expanding rings. They looked for signs of him on foot or horseback or something else, but all they found was the half-buried tracks of a half-tread truck.

Sally told Laura to stay at the ranch, but to keep searching wider and wider, to keep calling out her brother's name. She had to hope it was just him approaching his teenage years, that it was just him needing to wander, that it was just him out having an adventure in the wild. But in the world of Altadas, hope wasn't something you clung too tightly to. Hope with a capital H was the drug you took when the real hope had all dried up.

Sally travelled to her nearest neighbour, the Bucks Family, but she found them out on the fields on horses of their own. They asked her if she'd seen the young twins before she had a chance to ask about Luke. They told her that Young Widow West up by the mill was missing her daughter too. By now, it was clear as crystal, as right as rain, as sure as sand. None of them had gone off wandering. They'd been taken.

Sally raced back to Handcart Ranch to find Laura sitting despondently on the porch, her chin in her hands. Her face was covered with the tears of many different cries. Those later ones were drier tears.

"Did you—?" was all Laura could manage before Sally slung herself off her horse and brushed by in a haze. Laura had barely managed to wipe her face clean.

Sally went into the dining room and pushed aside the giant table. It didn't matter that she knocked over the candlesticks. It didn't matter that she scuffed one of the chairs. All that mattered now was time. Every second wasted meant Luke was taken farther and farther away.

Sally tore up the rug that covered a giant hatch leading to a secret storage space below. She unlocked the hinges with a clang and swung open the twin doors. Inside, in the deep, dark recess, was a tarpaulin sheet filled with electronic equipment. Some of it supposedly came from Codex Carter, a former spy for the Resistance, who maybe needed a new job after the fall of the Regime. But most of it came from the Coilhunter, including a large radio and an even larger antenna rig that needed to be put up on the roof.

Sally struggled to yank the equipment out and stumbled over as she did.

"Help me!" she yelled at Laura. She didn't mean to yell, but the anger and the fear festered in her and made itself into a terrible rage. All that she could do to hold it back was do anything else at all, anything that might bring that boy back to her.

The duo brought the equipment upstairs and laid it out on Luke's bed. His empty bed. The bed he should've been woken from that morning. The bed he should've been tucked into that night. He was maybe too much of a rebel now for that, too prideful to admit that he still wanted those comforts, too much of a "man" for his eleven years. And don't forget that one month. No, the gravestone wouldn't either.

They opened the windows leading onto the first-floor roof and carried the antenna rig outside. By now it was starting to rain, a rare sight in that dusty desert, and it came down heavy, like those withheld tears. But the weather wasn't crying with them. It was adding its salt-laced tears to put a little more sting in the wounds. Sally didn't want to think it, but she feared now that even if they got all of that machinery to work, the clouds would block the signal. She fought that fear like she fought her own tears.

"I don't think it'll hold!" Laura shouted as the wind and the rain picked up.

"It doesn't need to hold," Sally said. "Only for a moment."

"Then I'll hold it," Laura replied, and she hugged the chimney, pinning the antenna in place.

Any other time, Sally would've objected. Any other time, Sally would've said no. It was dangerous up there on that roof. It was dangerous up there in that weather. But Sally only needed a moment. She just hoped she'd get one.

She dived inside and messed with the radio dials. Nox had shown her how to do it, but that was a long time ago. This equipment was a backup and nothing more. They couldn't use it regularly for fear of attracting unwanted attention from the gangs—or worse.

All she heard was static. All she heard in the voice of her own mind was Luke's soft timbre, his pouting and his temper, and yet his politeness and his tenderness beneath it all. She hoped to a God she didn't believe in, and all those Devils she knew, that she wouldn't have to only remember his voice.

And then she had it. She heard the hum of another voice on the other end.

"Can you hear me?" she spoke into the microphone.

"Oh! You startled me, pumpkin!" came a familiar, high-pitched voice, with a little flavour and a little flair.

"Porridge," she said. "I need your help."

Chapter Thirty-four

ZONE DISSONANCE

Devilbane Higgins led the half-truck convoy through what felt like half the desert, but was barely just a few grains. For all their losses at Bellford, and all the commotion it caused, it felt like as easy a job as they'd ever done. But they shouldn't have smiled too broadly just yet. They should've known the Wild North never let you do anything easy at all.

"Somethin' on the road ahead," the driver said.

"Well, drive around it then," Devilbane Higgins replied. He didn't fancy being late. The Songsnatcher wasn't a patient sort, and though he was loath to admit it, he feared that man. Now, just imagine how the kids felt.

"It's ... a person."

"Well, drive *over* 'em then!" Devilbane Higgins urged.

The driver suddenly halted, almost sending Higgins from his seat. The children in the back cried and moaned as they banged their heads against the sides, or against each other. You could've said they were packed like sardines in there, but not many knew what sardines were in the Wild North. The seas were far-off, and fish were a luxury few could afford.

143

Now, sand was a different story. Yeah, they were packed like sand in there.

"I ... I think it's *him*," the driver said, almost whispering that last word, as if maybe it'd summon the Silent Silhouette, the Man Who Shines in the Shadows—the Coilhunter.

"It ain't—" But Devilbane Higgins paused. That dark shape out there, with the outline of a cowboy hat, with the shape of an oxygen tank on its back, and with hands down by its gun-holstered hips, well, it sure did look like him. But then sometimes the shadow of a cabinet looked like him. Sometimes the shape of a tree looked like him. Fear made you see things that weren't really there. Now, again—imagine how the kids felt.

"Go on out an' look," Devilbane Higgins told the driver.

"I ain't goin' out there!" the driver replied. You could've said most folk attracted to crime were rolling snake eyes for intelligence, but every so often they rolled doubles.

"Send one o' the guards then."

A lone guard was pushed out of the truck against his will. The other guards closed the back doors just as quick and hid there, shuddering with the children. Oh, you could be a brave man when snatching a child, but when the Coilhunter came for you, you shook like a child yourself. And maybe you even prayed for your momma.

The guard didn't walk out towards that figure. He inched out. Hell, he millimetred out. His gun trembled so much he might as well've left it behind.

But you needed something to hold on to then. Like maybe the hand of that momma of yours.

"W-who's out there?" he asked.

Oh, now you had to be careful asking something like that. There were a lot of devilish folk in the great "out there." Only one of them was the Nightcrawler. Only one of them was the Sheriff of the Shifting Sands. Only one of them was the Painted Badge.

There was no response, but that wasn't reassuring. *He* often came in silence. *He* often appeared without a sound. *He* often said nothing at all. Or he said it with gadgets. Or he said it with guns.

"You're blockin' the road," the guard said. He tried to say it a little braver, tried to hide the quiver in his voice, the shiver in his soul. But as veiled as that figure ahead was, the guard's fear wasn't veiled at all.

Devilbane Higgins sat and watched, rubbing his leather gloves together noisily, pressing them into that right leg of his that did a little involuntary jig every now and then. He knew the driver noticed, but then the driver's legs were dancing too.

The guard kept going, out and out, farther and farther into the darkness, where the figure ahead stood still and silent, waiting and watching, and maybe even drawing while they couldn't see.

Every second felt like a lifetime. They were all kids again, with time stretching out forever, but they were all old now too, like the elderly on their deathbeds, recounting their all-too-short lives, and wishing they'd done things differently, and wishing they'd done more. *He* made you think like that. The Redranger. The Toytinker. The Desert Bedmaker.

The guard reached the figure, and all watching grimaced. They expected the quick and abrupt blast of a gun. They expected the sharp and sudden explosion of light.

But nothing came.

The guard circled the figure, and then lifted one of its arms up and let it flop back down again.

"It's nothin' but a scarecrow!" he shouted back.

And then he keeled over to the side, dead as dirt, a little strawman of his own, and with the panic that followed, you could've called them all well-scared crows.

"Drive! Drive!" Devilbane Higgins shouted. The truck kicked into action, but already they heard the hum of the engine of the Coilhunter's fabled monowheel. It rolled right in front of the convoy, and there was the Masked Menace himself, standing one foot on the engine, one foot on the seat, both pistols raised towards the windows of the trucks ahead.

Boy did those bullets rain. The drivers that didn't dive were gunned down through the windshield, but Devilbane Higgins ducked for cover and used the body of his own driver as a human shield. Guess you didn't need a windshield at all.

The monowheel rolled on, and with it went the hail of lead. You might've thought it a fool's game to spray bullets like that, what with the children in the back, but the Coilhunter wasn't a careless shot.

And neither was Cactus Candy.

It wasn't a stray bullet that got the Coilhunter. It was a well-aimed one by that sharp-eyed, sharper-gunned woman, who didn't just believe in an eye for an eye, and a gun for a gun, but thought you should part with both of yours for one of hers. Well, she'd lost a brother, and the Coilhunter had none. Guess she'd have to settle for his life.

Chapter Thirty-five

THOSE FIGHTERS
YOU CALL FAMILY

Now, you knew that copper-plated copter any-where. If you didn't know it by sight, you knew it by sound. It chugged one moment, whizzed another, and clunked and clanked all the way through the heavens. It had several propellers across its globular surface, each of which kicked in and out of action seemingly at random, or rather when one conked out altogether. It also had globe windows to match, and the driver inside, strapped to his seat, zoomed around on a metal track that brought him to any given vantage point. You see, that copter, dubbed the Dandyman, was only reliable in the air because its maker had built so many backups into its scavenged-together form.

And the maker? Well, that was an eccentric trader and tinker known as Porridge.

The copter crash-landed into the corral at Hand-cart Ranch, sending the horses into a frenzy. Some of them bucked and kicked at the copper ball, while others cowered at the other end of their paddock, but they didn't need to be frightened of that vehicle or the man who drove it.

Porridge hobbled out in heels, purple and sparkling. When he regained his composure enough to almost pose by the doorframe, you got a better sense of the rest of his attire: skintight black leather trousers with pink and baby blue sequins down one leg, a bright yellow blouse with more frills than fabric, a blue and white-squared scarf that also became a cummerbund around his waist, and, to cover most of his brownish-blonde curls, a wide-brimmed straw hat with several small cacti nestled on top. It was quite the outfit, and it wasn't his only one.

Porridge found a large gathering of good folk waiting for him, some on horseback, like Sally and Laura, and good old Thomas Bucks of the Bucks Family. Others were townsfolk from nearby settlements, most of which weren't near at all. They'd gathered in numbers, because their children had been taken in numbers.

"Oh! Pardon me, plums," Porridge said as he strolled over. "But I do have to make an entrance! Oh, if only!"

"Who's this colourful chap?" Thomas Bucks asked.

"Porridge, dearie." He extended his hand like a baroness.

"Uh, like oatmeal?" Thomas asked, and he shook Porridge's hand awkwardly.

"Not quite as bland, blueberry, though I am quite good for you. Oh-hoh!"

Sally eyed him and shook her head. On any other occasion, she would've had time for this, but not now.

"Oh, I *am* sorry, honeyblossom," Porridge said.

"This is all a little too sombre for a poor old dandy like me. Oh, just terrible!"

"It ain't half as bad as what we're gonna do when we catch that Songsnatcher," Sally promised, and she said with the conviction of her former life of crime. They'd called her Handcart Sally then, and she buried the bodies the gangs didn't want anyone to find. She'd put that life behind her, but she'd bury one more body soon enough.

She just hoped it wouldn't be Luke.

Chapter Thirty-six

THE BALLAD OF THE MAN
WITH A THOUSAND NAMES

The way the Coilhunter went down, you thought he was done for. Why, you might've started writing that obituary of his. You might've started singing the funeral dirge. *Nathaniel Osley Xander*. Nox. The Man with a Thousand Names.

But you were wrong to rejoice just yet, if that was you clapping in the back. You see, the Coilhunter went down alright, and he went with a thud, but he didn't stay down. He came back blazing.

Nox halted the monowheel before him, half-hiding behind it for cover, and half-resting on it to prop him up. Cactus Candy had got him good, just below the ribcage. No doubt she was aiming a little higher, but he moved that "little" just in time. He now wished he'd moved a lot.

The pain didn't get you at first. The adrenaline did, and he was glad to have that. His eyes were wider than ever, taking in every little stir on the battlefield. He even spotted Cactus Candy beneath one of the trucks, splayed out and pointing that heartseeker of hers. He ducked and turned just in time for that bullet to ping off the metal plating of his guitar. Boy, it almost played his tune.

He pressed a button on his wristpad, which opened a panel on the side of his monowheel. A ramp extended, and out waddled a little toy duck. Now, that toy was yellow as the midday sun, and it might as well've had a target painted on it, because every single gun, including Cactus Candy's, turned to gun down that mechanical fowl as if it was hunting season. And Nox was counting on it. Because that's when he struck.

First came the blasting orbs. A dozen little balls rolled out in all directions, including under that truck where Cactus Candy hid. Some tried to swat or flick them away, but others ducked for cover, and others simply ran. Nox got his blackout goggles on just in time, knocking the shutter down tight.

The blasts of light weren't just blinding—they were burning. If you stared directly at them, you spent the next few minutes clawing your eyeballs. Even if you looked away, you were temporarily stunned, and your vision wouldn't return to normal before you were gunned down and buried.

Next came the butterfly canisters, which cracked open to reveal a horde of motion-seeking mechanical insects, and boy were there a lot of folk out there moving now. Many of them couldn't see well enough to spot the butterflies coming their way, but they felt their little claws, and smelled that noxious dream-inducing gas. Yes, the Coilhunter could send you to slumber too.

Nox used this downtime for a quick bit of wound cleansing. He opened one of his belt pouches and pulled a pliers out, along with a biting stick. He opened his mask and chewed that wood as he prodded around his torso until he found the bullet, then yanked it out with a muffled cry. He threw half a canister of whiskey over the wound, slapped on a sticky bandage, and holstered up for round two.

That was when he heard the skid of a motorcycle behind him. He turned to find Johnny Grin there, with a broad smile to match Nox's broader frown. Just what he needed. "Backup."

Chapter Thirty-seven

ONE TARGET, TWO GUNS

"Well, the sandworm spits twice," Johnny Grin said. "Though I probably should've guessed it was you, with all the wreckage an' all."

Nox couldn't help but sigh. "I'm startin' to think *you're* the Songsnatcher."

"Hey, and I'm startin' to think you are too. Maybe folk are right about you."

"Now, which folk are *you* talkin' to? You see, it's usually the criminals who talk like that."

Johnny Grin shrugged. "That's more than half o' folk out here. So, what you got here anyway? Looks like a field o' eyegrabbers. They been on the eyeboxes in the Burg? Keep tellin' folk they ain't no good. It's Hope you want if you want a *real* kick."

Nox grumbled, but ignored him. He limped on out to the abandoned trucks, glancing between each of them to find Cactus Candy. Here and there he slammed a door into the face of a criminal whose sight was returning. And here and there he slammed a bullet into one whose legs were working off into the distance. But there was no Cactus Candy. And no Devilbane Higgins. But that didn't mean there was no fish in the net.

154

"Well, look who we have here," Nox rasped, as he kicked over the body of Cactus Cody. He was still alive, but he held his eyes as if he'd been shot there. In a way, he had. He was one of the best sharpshooters there was, just like his sister, but you couldn't shoot anything if you couldn't see.

That youth bawled when he saw the hazy shimmer of the Coilhunter before him.

"Let me go! Let me live!" he begged, with the kind of desperation that told you he expected that the Coilhunter wouldn't let him do much of anything at all.

"Unlike your master," Nox croaked, "I don't kill kids."

"He's right there," Johnny Grin said, nudging up beside him like a sidekick. Oh, Nox wanted to kick him alright. "Haven't seen 'im kill a kid yet," Johnny continued. "But there's still time."

Now, that just made Cactus Cody reach for his pistol, but the Coilhunter kicked it away from him just in time.

"Don't make him right," he warned.

But that was the thing about the Wild North's youth, and the Wild North's old. You could warn once with words, and they wouldn't listen. Guess how you warned them the second time.

Cactus Cody reached for his other pistol, but Nox reached his own first. He blasted a hole right through the youth's hand, and boy did that boy scream.

"But you said!" Cactus Cody whined as he nursed the wound.

"I said I won't kill ya, but I ain't ever said anything

'bout not hurtin' ya. You'll live, boy. For now. If you've got any pink stuff in that head o' yours, you'll change your ways and maybe you'll live tomorrow too."

"You're a monster!" Cody yelled at him. Johnny Grin thought about it for a moment and nodded in agreement.

"Well, maybe I am, but I'm a necessary one," Nox croaked. "Tell me, boy. How necessary are you?"

"Oh, don't he give you the shivers," Johnny Grin said, taking more than a little sting out of those words, and more than a little shiver. He was becoming quite the nuisance. But it wasn't a crime to be a nuisance, even if right now Nox wished it was.

Nox slapped a snake rope around Cactus Cody, who cursed every one of Nox's thousand names. Well, at least the ones he could remember. Nox thought he heard a few new ones for good measure. Eyeblinder and Handblaster made their way through the curses to his ears.

"You," Nox said to Johnny Grin, "go release the kids."

"Oh, is that what this is? A rescue mission? Thought we were after the Songsnatcher."

"*I* am. There ain't no *we*."

"You sure 'bout that? You look like you could do with a nurse. I happen to be handy with the ol' splint and white lace."

"Well, put on that apron and nurse those kids then."

"Whatever you say, boss. Just, y'know, holler if you keel over."

Johnny Grin went away then and started unload-

156

ing the trucks. Nox was never so glad to be rid of him, but he didn't mind the help rescuing the kids. It freed him up to find the perpetrators. Right now, he knew they must still be there amidst the rubble. No one was getting anywhere on foot.

Johnny did a mighty good job getting those kids out, from the sound of things, but then Nox realised that the No-gun Marshals had caught up with them and were doing most of the work. Johnny spent more time rooting through the pockets of some of the criminals, and lightning up a scavenged cigarette.

Nox continued his search, until suddenly he heard Johnny Grin yell "Hey!" as one of the trucks fired up. Nox turned to see the bounty hunter scrambling to pull the last kid from the back as the vehicle started to roll off. That was when Nox ran right in front of it, eyeballed Devilbane Higgins at the wheel, and fired a grapnel right through the windshield.

The truck halted just as suddenly and Nox reeled that criminal in like a fish, pulling him out of his seat, onto the bonnet, and then back down to the dirt where he belonged. He tried to play dead there for a moment, but Nox was going to show him how to be the real thing.

"Ya got me," Devilbane Higgins said, as the Coilhunter kicked him onto his back.

"I got ya."

"Maybe we can come to some kinda compromise?" Devilbane Higgins proposed.

"Sure," Nox rasped. "You don't want me to kill ya and I do. So, let's compromise and you can do it yourself."

"That ... that's not what I mean!"

"Well, a deal's a deal, even to a criminal like you. So tell me, Devilbane. How ya gonna do it?"

"I ... uh..."

"Is it gonna be by the rope? 'Cause I brought me my lasso."

"Please..."

"Or maybe you like lead. Your gun or mine?"

"I'll do anything!"

"Or perhaps you wanna go out in fire or fireworks. Somethin' unorthodox. Hey, I ain't judgin'. I'm just here to watch ya burn."

Now, the convicts and conmen of the world all said the same thing: they'd go down gunning or not at all. But when it came to it, when it came to them facing the Coilhunter in their final hours, so many of them went down crying instead. You'd almost pity them, if they had any for anyone else. So you saved your compassion, and you named your pistol Pity, and you gave them plenty of that instead.

Devilbane Higgins bawled up the barrel of the Coilhunter's gun. "Please!" he begged, like a child. Like all those children he'd captured or led to the cage.

"You call yourself Devilbane," Nox drawled, "and there's a devil out there alright called the Songsnatcher. You be his bane and I won't be yours. You lead me to 'im and maybe I won't lead you to the doors o' that other Devil in the land below."

Chapter Thirty-eight

THE BATTLE OF
STICK AND SONG

Devilbane Higgins was a religious man, a man of morals and values, though not necessarily the same morals and values of others of his church. He believed that there was a devil in everyone which had to be resisted, which meant he took to the teachings about the so-called demons like a duck to water— or a mechanical duck to sand. Of course, some folk pointed out that if there was a devil in everyone, there must also be a devil in him. Like most criminals, he was the bane of himself.

Despite his values, and how much the Songsnatcher seemed to espouse and enhance them, Devilbane Higgins was also a practical man, a man of survival, and if that meant trading in some morals, then it was time for a little code of honour commerce. You'd be surprised what you could buy and sell in the Wild North. But then if there was a devil in everyone, you shouldn't be that surprised that it'd start by selling your soul.

"If you're lyin'—" Nox began, but Devilbane Higgins cut him short.

"I know, I know," he said. "I'm a man o' my word."

"A man of honour, huh?" Nox asked. "Sellin' out his master. Funny, that."

"It'll only be funny if you get 'im. This might be the death o' me."

"Then maybe I can cash you in both."

Devilbane Higgins directed the requisitioned convoy, filled now with the Coilhunter, the No-gun Marshals, and Johnny Grin, through the Barrens, vast empty stretches of desert leading from east to west, flat and featureless for miles. Most folk never came here, except maybe to die, and most animals didn't either, except maybe to kill them. It meant those trucks stood out like a sore thumb, like maybe one that'd spent too much time cocking hammers. Oh, you could already feel the air tensing up as they got nearer.

The destination site was almost as empty as the rest, except for a little campsite with tribal tents. You could see it from the distance, but you wouldn't have made much of it except for that figure that stood there waiting, and watching through a double eyeglass.

There he was. The Songsnatcher.

He wore large, shapeless steel armour, and a full face-mask, covering even his hair. He hunched a little, but stood solid, like a man who'd held the weight of the world for far too many years. In one way, he was stronger because of it, and in another, he was weakened by it too.

"I guess you ain't him then," Nox said to Johnny Grin beside him.

"Told you I wasn't. Guess you ain't either."

"The real guess," Eleanor "No-gun" Pickett said,

"is whether or not we can take 'im."

The Songsnatcher wasn't expecting those half-tread trucks to contain the Coilhunter, Johnny Grin, and the No-gun Marshals, but he extended his singlesticks all the same. He had just the two of them, but something told the Coilhunter that in a close quarters fight, he might only need the one.

The Songsnatcher was more than outnumbered. Even if he managed to take down half of his attackers, he was still a guaranteed lockup, and that was a guarantee everyone there was glad to cash in on. Oh, you could hear the clink of coils already.

But don't you forget where you were. This was the Wild North, after all. There were no such things as guarantees, except maybe the scald of the sun, the sting of the scorpion, and the itch of the sand. Everything else was dice and cards, and even when the black-legs made sure the dice were loaded and the cards were stacked, chance'd find a way to surprise you. Nox always said he was no gambler, but in the Wild North, life was the greatest gamble of them all.

"Give it up," Nox said, as he flexed his fingers over his holsters. He had no singlesticks, but he did have a pair of pistols locked and loaded. "We've got you surrounded. There ain't anywhere for you to run."

"You're overconfident, Coilhunter," the Song-snatcher said, and he said it with a voicebox, which made his words come out a little robotic. It wasn't clear if it was to disguise his voice or if he really needed it to speak.

"Well, maybe I am," Nox replied, "but I'm just the right amount of confident that now or later I'm gonna get ya. And that ain't over or under, boy."

"And that's where you're wrong again, Coilhunter. I ain't no boy. And if I were, then I'd be a demon too."

"Well, let's not discount that quite yet," Nox said.

"Give me a shot at 'im," Eleanor "No-gun" Pickett proposed.

"I don't let anyone take my kills."

"I won't be killin' 'im. Just, ya know, roughin' 'im up."

"Well, that I can allow."

"You can try," the Songsnatcher said, "but your skills are no match for me. See, you learned for law. I learned for justice. Only one of those keeps you up trainin' at night. Only one of those fuels you when the bread runs low. Only one of those gives you fire when the sun fades."

"Enough poetry," Eleanor said, before charging in with fists of prose.

Now, that was a sight to behold. Eleanor "No-gun" Pickett more than lived up to her name. Her first move was a flying kick, which the Songsnatcher batted to the side with both of his singlesticks. Those blows should've broken Eleanor's leg, but she was well-conditioned to forceful strikes. She didn't fall, but roll, and she was back on her feet just as quick, and launched a flurry of blows with her hands even quicker. Yet each of these the Songsnatcher parried, and he moved only a little for each of her greater gestures.

Then there was a pause in the fight as Eleanor pulled back to regroup, and the Songsnatcher stood with his singlesticks down to his sides, like a gunslinger waiting to draw.

"Who trained you?" Eleanor asked him.

"I have many masters," the Songsnatcher said. "Anger is my mentor. Pain is my trainer. Sufferin' is my tutor. You learned your art from the livin', Eleanor. I learned mine from life."

Eleanor charged in again, with faster and harsher blows, and the Songsnatcher was forced to exert more effort to block them this time, yet still seemed to stop them with ease. To anyone watching, several of Eleanor's attacks would've felled bigger foes than this one, but the Songsnatcher was faster, and stayed forever standing.

Nox had a go at correcting that.

With his own fast hands, he drew both his pistols and fired a bullet from each straight for the Songsnatcher's skull. To his surprise, the man shifted position to dodge one and bashed away the other with his singlesticks. Nox had never seen anything like it before, and couldn't help but feel like maybe the Songsnatcher wasn't wrong about his overconfidence.

It was then that the rest of the No-gun Marshals charged in, and then the battle grew fiercer and more violent. The Songsnatcher turned this way and that, parrying blows here, kicking away an attacker there. He couldn't halt every hit, but his armour was thick, so even those that landed didn't stop him like they would've stopped others.

Johnny Grin sauntered up to the Coilhunter. "You'd almost pay to see this," he said.

"We might still," Nox said. "But what're you waitin' for? There's a bounty to cash."

In almost rehearsed swiftness, both bounty hunters drew their pistols and fired into the fray, but this time the Songsnatcher didn't just dodge and parry. He pulled one of the No-gun Marshals into the line of fire, using her as a human shield.

And then, just as all hands joined the battle, and it seemed like the Songsnatcher didn't have enough hands of his own to stop them, he pulled a flute from his belt and brought it to his lips. Fists came in towards him as he played, as he left openings for stronger attacks, as he left no defence against the blows. But just as they were about to land, as they were about to topple the Songsnatcher, the No-gun Marshals heard that haunting, otherworldly tune, and one by one they fell backwards into a deep and overpowering slumber.

Nox managed to pull on a pair of noise-cancelling earmuffs just in time, though he heard the opening notes and felt immediately a little woozy, as if maybe he'd spent too long at the bar and caught a bit of barrel fever. Johnny Grin, on the other hand, was well and truly in the barrel.

The criminal had been outnumbered, but now it was even, the Songsnatcher and the Wrongcatcher. All bets were off, and yet the Wild North kept betting.

Nox fired, and he got his mark good, but to his surprise, the bullet pinged off the Songsnatcher's armour.

"Damn," Nox said, before the Songsnatcher charged in, slid to the ground as he came in, and knocked the Coilhunter off his feet with a scissors kick. Then he circled his legs and was back standing before Nox had even gotten to his knees.

`The first bash of a singlestick almost broke his forearm. He'd managed to brace for it just in time. The next got his shoulder, and he barely had time to groan before the first struck him in the side where Cactus Candy got him good. Oh, the Songsnatcher got him gooder. It was as if every weakness, every opening, was magnified. All Nox could do was try to block the blows.

The strikes came in hard and fast, far faster than anything Nox had experienced in the past. He'd had his fair share of fistfights with the boisterous barflies and the overconfident criminals, but this was something else. This was someone who was *trained*, and it was training unlike anything Nox had seen before.

Nox was forced to use his wristpads and grapnel launchers for a little extra protection from the blows. He could hear them crunching beneath the whacks of the wooden poles. He even heard them chirp and beep as the Songsnatcher inadvertently hit some of the buttons, sending one grapnel out into nowhere, and calling up the monowheel into tracking mode, and his mechanical owl back to scout.

The monowheel zoomed towards them, even as Nox was bashed down to the ground, with strike after strike against the backs and sides of his knees. The pain was unbearable, and for a moment he wondered if he'd ever be able to walk again. And then, as the monowheel came in for its ninepin kill, the Songsnatcher wasn't bowled over, but jumped inside, and turned it so fast that it whacked Nox right in the chin and sent him out cool. Oh, he was still semi-conscious, and could get colder. The Songsnatcher swapped his singlesticks for a pistol to do just that.

"There's a higher law," his voice crackled like radio static. "You, of all people, should know that."

"I do," Nox coughed, and he spat up some blood. "That's why I hunted you."

"Well, yours is over. But I still have many to hunt." The Songsnatcher aimed that pistol, almost half-reluctantly, as if he somehow respected the Coilhunter's plight, as if maybe he saw in him a kind of comrade of justice, someone out for the good fight, even if they just happened to be fighting on opposite sides. Well, you could respect your enemy, but your gun only respected your finger. Time to get clicking then.

That was it. Nox was finally done for.

Until Chance Oakley arrived.

Chapter Thirty-nine

A CHANCE TO REST

Chance Oakley was a drifter, and there was plenty of space in the Wild North to drift, but he had an uncanny way of drifting right into the path of trouble—or the place of necessity. He said everyone deserved a second chance, and he found his way of giving them one. It was lucky for Nox he did, because it was only that reason that Nox lived that day.

When the Songsnatcher saw Chance Oakley's silhouette on the horizon, riding that augmented horse of his, dubbed Old Reliable, he put his pistol away, gave a tip of his bolero hat, which Oakley gave in return, and drove off on the Coilhunter's monowheel. By the time Oakley trotted up to Nox and hauled him to his groggy feet, the Songsnatcher was well and truly gone.

"G'day, Coilhunter," Oakley said.

"It ain't a good day," Nox replied. "You let 'im get away."

"I let you live, more like," Oakley said. "A second chance for life, and maybe a second chance at catchin' 'im."

"Why'd he let me go? He had me good there."

"Lord, I can't rightly say, but I've gotten more

than my fair share of nods and hat tips from folk here and there, and more often than not it meant I'd given 'em a second chance some time before that no one else would. So, they were just repayin' the favour. Only reason I'm still alive, I wager. Not that I'm the wagerin' type, mind."

"Well, if that's the case, we just used your second chance card," Nox said. "I can't imagine he'll give us a third."

"Few even give the second one," Oakley admitted.

Nox looked around at the battlefield, where all of the combatants except him were dozing.

"That flute of his is somethin' else," he said. "We can't even fight 'im if he puts us to sleep."

Oakley patted Old Reliable, who whinnied playfully. That sorrel had seen a lot with his master, and with Nox, and had the two mechanical front legs to prove it. A field of sleeping soldiers was small sand compared to everything else.

"Looks like somethin' from the Apanajos, if I'm not mistaken," Oakley said. "I know many of the tribes well, but I thought the Apanajos were extinct. Other tribes talk of it. They say the only song playin' now is a song of endin'. That music should've died with 'im, mind."

"It clearly hasn't," Nox said, "or someone's done a deadwalker and brought it back to life."

Oakley sighed deeply. "Lord, not the first time, true enough. Makes you wonder about life and death, and what it's all about."

"I ain't no philosopher," Nox replied. "I'll leave the wonderin' and wanderin' to you. I'll do the huntin' and the killin', and right now there's only one man in my sights."

It was nightfall before the others came to, despite Oakley's use of a wide range of smelling salts. He had quite the collection, with many strange concoctions he'd gathered in his travels. He had at least one mix from each of the tribes, even the unfriendly ones. You see, Oakley had a way of making a friend out of everyone. Second chances came in handy then.

Johnny Grin took his not-so-graceful defeat on the chin, where he had a cut from his fall for good measure. He cracked open his whiskey flask and cigar case and passed both around. If someone was going to force him to rest, he wasn't going to fight that at all.

Eleanor "No-gun" Pickett was more frustrated than most. It was one thing being outgunned, but being outarmed and outlegged was something else. That was her arena, and she'd just found a better fighter. Folk said pride bruises bluer than blood, and she was azure.

"Those moves o' his," Nox said as he gave an awkward demonstration. "I ain't ever seen anything like it."

"It's the same moves as ours," Eleanor replied, "but with weapons. He had to have gotten trainin' in *askarochi*, and we definitely didn't give it. We trained no men."

"Can you train me?"

"You want to be our exception, huh?"

"Only if I can be exceptional."

"That would take months or years."

"You've got hours."

"It can't be done, Coilhunter."

"Just give me the counters. Enough to not be surprised by him again."

"We don't train men," Eleanor insisted.

"Then train a phantom," Nox crooned. "Train a shadow. Train *me*."

Chapter Forty

INTO WILDER LANDS

They set out the next day, not, as Johnny Grin wanted, on the trail of the Songsnatcher, who went south, but north to tribal territory again, following Chance Oakley's suggestion to find the Sage of Ages of the Machu Muada, the Mother-tribe. It was she, Oakley said, that would know the most about the lost music of the Apanajo tribe. Nox just hoped that information wasn't lost to her too. This was a detour he wasn't keen to make, but he knew he couldn't face the Songsnatcher again until he was better armed—and better with his arms too.

The journey took several days, because the Mother-tribe was nestled in the heart of tribal lands, with the other tribes acting like a protective barrier around them. Some sent scouts to intercept them, but when they saw Oakley, they allowed them to pass. He showed many tokens and trinkets of friendship to those who didn't know him personally, and they said "You are known to us" in their tongue.

They rested each nightfall, and Eleanor "No-gun" Pickett used that time to train Nox in some of the basics of her art. He was a quick learner, but he was no natural. Folk said nature only gave you one gift, and Northfolk said that nature would use everything else to take it away. Having two gun arms was a boon few could boast about, and Nox used that gift well, but a singlestick to the wrists was all it took to take that advantage away. It was time to even the odds.

The land of the Mother-tribe was as verdant as much of the world of Altadas was in bygone times, but it'd retained all of its beauty. It rained frequently there, unlike most of the Wild North, and it was raining when Oakley's oddballs arrived. Tribesfolk tended to crops and animals, preparing carts to send out to the other tribes, and down south to the "walled ones," the so-called "civilised folk" who spent much of their time stealing and murdering to make a living. The tribesfolk would've said you can't make a living by taking a life.

The Sage of Ages was, to Nox's surprise, not an old man or old woman, but a child. She was small of frame, with black hair plaited together and tied into an ornate pattern, like the interlocking branches of a tree. She sat cross-legged in her potato-sack dress on the stump of an old oak tree, said to be the wisest of all woods. Nox was no treehugger by any stretch, and the Wild North had few of them to hug, but right now he was willing to listen to wisdom from anyone or anything. Even a child. Even a tree. Indeed, it was perhaps fitting that a child might have the answers to save other children. Or maybe it was only time before this kid was in a cage too.

"Oh great Sage," Chance Oakley said, as he took off his hat and bowed his head. "I bring some fellow drifters in search o' answers."

"I have foreseen it," the girl said. "One Who Embodies Law."

"I think that's you," Johnny Grin said, nudging Nox with his elbow. "Though it could be me also. Y'know, when I finish takin' your job an' all. Just sayin'."

"You seek Music of Songsouls," the girl continued.

"The Songsouls?" Nox asked.

"The Apanajo," Oakley explained.

"Oldest tribe," the girl said. "They heard First Song."

"Hope it had drums," Johnny Grin said. "Can't beat some good bongos."

"Are they gone?" Nox asked. "I searched their lands and found nothin'."

"Did you listen?" the Sage asked.

"As good as any gunslinger."

"So not very then."

Johnny Grin had to stifle a laugh. "Oh, I like this one."

"I ain't no tribesman," Nox said.

"All belong to tribe," the girl said.

"Even drifters," Oakley added.

She nodded. "Even drifters."

"I need to know how to defeat the Songsnatcher," Nox said. "He's usin' that music o' yours to trap and kill the innocent."

"Defiler," the Sage said, nodding again. "There are many."

"Not like this one."

"So your guns did not defeat them?"

"No," Nox admitted.

"And your devices did not defeat them?"

"No."

"And your fists did not defeat them?"

"No."

The girl nodded more and more to each and every answer in the negative, clearly well aware that none of those methods would work.

"They attack with music," she said. "So you must defend with some."

Chapter Forty-one

THE RHYTHM OF
THE ANCIENTS

The tribesfolk spoke of song as being the voice of the ancestors. They said you never sang alone. They said there was always a spirit chorus. For some, that was comforting. For others, it made their skin crawl. Well, whether you were comfortable or not, you certainly weren't alone.

The Sage of Ages made a small, almost imperceptible gesture, and two of the meditating tribesfolk far behind stood up immediately in answer. They left the area and came back with a *bodhrán*, a large flat frame drum, which had been modelled like his guitar and covered in metal plating. It was almost as if it was made for him.

The carriers handed it to the girl, who offered it to Nox in turn.

"What is it?" Nox asked.

"Sonic shield."

"Let me guess," Johnny Grin said. "It protects against music."

"In its own way, yes."

"How?" Nox asked.

The girl approached Nox and put out her hands.

"Your six-string."

Nox reluctantly unstrapped his buckled guitar and handed it over to her. It looked huge in her hands.

She walked away, cradling the instrument like a child. Then she turned, pointed the neck of the six-string at Nox, formed a chord unlike anything he'd ever seen before—where her hand joints seemed to almost elongate and reach the top and bottom frets simultaneously—and then hammered and strummed those strings like he played his guns.

The music was like a hurricane.

Something invisible came from that guitar, just like his secret smoke chamber, and struck him in the chest. He was bowled over by it and had to be helped up by Oakley and Eleanor.

"This is discord," the Sage explained. "From Second Song, the Song of Endings."

"And how do I end it?" Nox asked.

"You must use sonic shield to play *morendo*," she said.

"To die away," Oakley said, remembering the musical term from his youth.

"But I don't know the music," Nox said.

"You do," the girl replied. "Land taught it to you."

"I don't understand."

And that was when she played his tune.

Chapter Forty-two

BACK TO THE HUNT

The journey back to the familiar sands seemed shorter than the way up, but it was spent in much the same way, travelling by foot and horseback, exchanging stories over a campfire, and training for the battle to come.

On one campfire chat, Chance Oakley pulled out a vinegar pie from his supplies and divvied it up between the group. Good apples were a tribesfolk delicacy, but good old apple cider vinegar was something the likes of Oakley could trade for, and he made a mean pie with pastry and that tart liquid. Even Nox, who shied away from eating with others, couldn't resist the sweet smell as it roasted brown over the fire. A few took a peek at his scars as he ate.

"I can't quite fathom it," Oakley said, referring to the Songsnatcher's mission. "I never did buy into the whole demon claim for those outsiders, mind, not when the war was ragin' and even less now that it's over. I met some once, and we shared a campfire just like this one. They called themselves *marans*, and they thought we were just as strange as we thought they were."

"You're a good cook," Johnny Grin said, "but an

even better evangelist for that way o' thinkin' o' yours. Here, give us another slice and make me a true believer."

"I know some who lost their babies when they came," Eleanor "No-gun" Pickett said. She stared at the fire, as if maybe she could see the souls of the unborn burning there. "So, I'm not sure what to believe."

"Surely you don't believe in killin' the young," Nox said.

"No, definitely not," Eleanor replied, "but I can understand why some believe it." She tried not to glance at Helen "All-arms" Clanton to her left, who in turn tried not to glance at any of the others.

"Whatever folk believe," June "Four-fist" Fisher said, "I think we can all agree that what the Song-snatcher's doin' is wrong. And we've gotta stop 'im."

They all nodded and mumbled their agreement with a mouthful of pie. Nox nodded more than most. It was at times like this, around a fire like that, that he couldn't help but think of his family. Despite all those people around him, he never felt so alone.

"Never did have any little ones o' my own," Oakley said. "Often did wonder 'bout it. I mean, is this even the right world for 'em? Maybe it'd be better for 'em elsewhere—through one o' them portals, or across that western sea to where the Magi come from. Iraldas, they call it?"

"So they say," Johnny Grin commented. "But I think that was all just parlour tricks."

"You're new here, Johnny," Nox rasped. "Stay a while longer and you'll believe the man who saws women in half is really doin' the sawin'."

"Or the man who makes kids disappear ain't doin' tricks either," Eleanor added.

"Lord help us," Oakley said. "In a world like this, what are we even fightin' for?"

"For them," Nox said. "For the rest of 'em. All of 'em. Everywhere. Human. Demon." He scoffed. "They ain't nothin' but kids. You don't condemn them for bein' young. And you don't judge 'em for bein' born in Hell."

Chapter Forty-three

PURGATORY

When Luke awoke, he wasn't sure where he was. His head swam, but his thoughts were little fishes he couldn't quite catch yet. It took him a good while to adjust to his surroundings, for his eyes to make out the bars before him, for his hands to really feel that damp stone beneath him, for his back to really feel those hard walls behind him.

"Howdy," came a young voice in the cell next to him. Luke flinched, like he did when he was first captured by the Night Slavers more than a year before, but he quickly replaced that involuntary action with the voluntary one of false courage. You could only have your small allotment of the real kind, but for the false stuff, you could have as much as you liked, and as much as everyone else would buy. That other little boy in the cell next to him hadn't a coil to spare.

"It's okay to be scared," he said.

"I ain't scared," Luke instinctively replied, with anger and hurt in his voice. He heard the words of his sister, her accusing voice, and yet her comforting voice too. He'd said he hated her only a few days ago. How he hated he'd said that now. How he hated that she might believe it too.

"What's your name?" the boy asked him. He came closer, and held one of the bars between their cells with one hand, while extending his thin arm through the gap in an offer of friendship. He was younger than Luke by a good four or five years, and was very small, and had brown curly hair and freckled cheeks. And, despite where he was, he had a smile.

Luke hesitated. He hadn't revealed his name to the Night Slavers either, but they'd read it on his belongings, which they'd taken from him. He couldn't help that sliver of defiance in him, something the slavers couldn't take.

"Noah Walker," the boy said, offering his name first. Now, wasn't that a kindness. Or maybe it was a cruelty in disguise, a hidden trap, a way to lure him in. Luke had become more and more jaded over the years. Hell, over the months. The Wild North did a number on everyone eventually, and boy was it doing a number on him.

"It's awful lonely here," Noah said despondently, now resting his head against the bars and letting his arms swing through. "I thought ... I thought maybe you'd want to talk."

"I don't."

"Oh, well, okay."

They sat in silence for a moment. Luke looked around to see any sign of food or water. His belly was growling now, as if it wanted to talk instead. His throat was dry and coarse, and he wanted to cough, but fought back the urge, as if somehow that'd give him away too.

Noah tried to whistle to himself, but wasn't really

good at it. Not everyone was the musical type. Not everyone was the Songsnatcher.

"Luke Mayfield," Luke said in time.

"Hmm?"

"My name."

"Oh, well, howdy Luke Mayfield." Noah took off his hat, which was far too big for him, and gave as polite a nod as any boy had ever made. If he was there to trick him, he was really good at it. Or, maybe, just maybe, he was a victim too.

Chapter Forty-four

BULLDOZER SALLY

Sally's posse trekked through half the desert looking for the Songsnatcher's trail. They went through towns and villages, asking for sight or hear of him, and got closer in some places and farther in others. Eventually, after Porridge spotted the Coilhunter's stolen and abandoned monowheel from his copter, they found their way out to a newly-built stone building out in the middle of nowhere, which some folk likened to a prison.

"I hope this is it," Thomas Bucks said. His wife, Mary, was the silent, brooding type, and she brooded plenty on his arm. It seemed like she mightn't say anything again if she didn't get her twins back. She sure didn't want to get her hopes up. She was a Wild North woman after all.

"Look for an entrance," Sally said, "but be careful. Who knows what they have here."

And she was right.

Porridge yelped and almost fell over. Laura ran to his aid, as did a few of the others, thinking he'd stood on a mine. Instead, his heel had caught in a cowpat. "Oh, my ripened raspberries! That'll never come out."

"Why, the surface coal's everywhere," Thomas

Bucks observed. "This must've been a farm before it was converted into … whatever this is."

They circled the building, which was larger than they thought from afar, but couldn't see any sign of an entrance.

"A house with no door," Sally said. "If that ain't suspicious, then I don't know what is."

"Oh, how are we going to get through, honeyblossom?" Porridge asked. He bashed his fist at the wall, though *bash* might've been an exaggeration. It was more of a gentle, well-rehearsed tap.

That was when Sally pulled back the caparison from her horse, revealing pack after pack of strapped dynamite.

"Oh!" Porridge exclaimed. "And you rode that thing?"

"Get back," Sally said, as she set the sticks in place. No one else offered to help her, and she wasn't the type to accept that help. Besides, she knew how to rig a place to blow. The Coilhunter had learned that about her early on.

They got as far away as possible and hid behind whatever cover they could find, which wasn't much. Then Sally set the charge, and that wall boomed and crumbled.

"We're in!" Porridge cried, but they weren't in just yet. You see, you could knock on the door of your enemy, or you could sneak on in, and, well, this was one hell of a way of knocking. The Songsnatcher's guards streamed out in numbers.

The dynamite had done its job. Now it was time for good old guns.

Thomas Hicks took out the first guard with his rifle, but he was slow to reload. Sally and Laura took out several others before they had a chance to take him out instead. Porridge used a tiny hand pistol, painted pink, though he spent more time popping up and down from behind his rock, taking aim and then hiding again before he'd taken his shot.

And then a bullet clipped through Porridge's hat, blasting off one of the cacti on top.

"My cactus!" he cried. He held the hat before him like a wounded comrade, placed a hand on his heart as if he was silently reciting an obituary, and then stood up tall and blasted that pink pistol at every guard in sight. Then he dropped back down again and panted loudly. "Oh! This is too much excitement for me."

In time, the gunfire went from a regular stutter to a periodic stammer, and then to a lone shot, and then to nothing at all. They waited for a moment after that. You could've said they were waiting for Death to stroll through the bodies on the other side, making sure they were dead. Oh, he'd make sure of that.

When they were certain the way was clear, they gathered up and entered the new door they'd made in the building, keeping each other close, and their guns closer. It was immediately clear, once they were in, that the previous entrance had been walled up from the inside. It seemed they knew that the law was coming for them and they were preparing to bunker down. Well, just as well Sally had brought her bunker-busters.

They tiptoed through the dimly-lit corridors,

listening to the eerie silence. Every room they passed looked empty, except for some supplies here and there. It seemed like the Songsnatcher's people hadn't gotten to finish what they started there, which was either very good or very bad. The entire place had the vibe of a torture chamber, but there were no obvious signs of torture. Oh, but it was torturing their minds something fierce.

In time, they reached what looked like an entrance to another level, deep beneath the dirt. Most folk had them in the Wild North, what with the sandstorms and the constant threat of war, but you couldn't help but feel like going down there was like entering the grave. But maybe you were just paying a visit. And maybe you were just picking out the best spot.

"Whatever happens here," Sally said, "we fight."

Laura nodded and hugged her rifle.

Thomas Bucks held his wife close, but kept his pistol cocked.

Porridge bit his knuckles in anticipation.

The others with them were ready too.

And then Sally placed her hand on the handle of that door and pulled it down. It creaked open slowly and noisily, revealing another dark room behind. Except that dark room had an even darker shape inside.

"Welcome," the Songsnatcher said. "You're a bit older than my other guests, but I still prepared you a room."

They tried to raise their guns, but the Songsnatcher raised his flute all the faster. He played that haunting, otherworldly tune, which threatened to bring them there, and they fell one-by-one to the ground, many on top of the rifles they'd aimed. Oh, they were lucky they didn't pull the trigger then.

See, it didn't matter if you had a bulldozer if what you were knocking through cut out your engine. But Sally and her posse wouldn't quite know that yet until they awoke, and where they'd awake was anyone's guess. Those new guards that streamed in and dragged their bodies down to the basement probably had a real good idea.

Chapter Forty-five

SNATCHED

When Sally came to, she found herself with all the others, dumped into a cage far too small for the amount of them. It was clearly made for a child, but the Songsnatcher was adapting to whomever came his way. Sally expected to fight. Hell, she even expected to die. She didn't, however, expect to be snatched.

Some of the others were already awake, while some were still dozing. That music had a slightly different effect on everyone. Maybe it depended on your physical stature. Or maybe it depended on your state of mind. Hell, maybe it depended on your taste in song.

"Where are we?" Sally asked.

"Can't quite tell," Thomas Bucks replied, "but it looks like we're down one or two levels. Looks like folk weren't wrong about this bein' a prison."

"Oh! I'm done for!" Porridge cried. "I'm not meant to be caged up like this. I'm a beautiful bird that's meant to fly! Oh, they've clipped my wings too soon, daffodil, too soon. Oh!"

Mary Bucks consoled him like her husband consoled her.

"Did they leave us anything?" Sally asked.

"Not much," Thomas Bucks said. "They took our guns."

"They took my hat," Porridge said with tears in his eyes. He placed his fist up to his mouth to stop himself bawling. Mary Bucks had one hell of a job to do.

"And they took our food," Thomas Bucks continued, "and there's none here that we can see."

No one was hungry yet, but they would be soon enough if they stayed in that cell. The Songsnatcher had prepared a room for them alright, but he hadn't prepared their meals. Folk said you needed three square meals a day. Or, well, you could take a round and not have to eat at all.

"The other cages are empty," Sally observed.

"I'm guessin' the Songsnatcher didn't get a chance to fill 'em yet," Thomas Bucks said. "It seems maybe we foiled his plan."

"Some foil," Porridge complained. He grabbed a hold of the bars and yelled, "Let me out! *Oh!*"

A guard came by and rapped his singlestick on Porridge's fingers, forcing his hands back inside.

"Ow! There's no need for that, peach. I'm just practising my voice!"

"Well, don't."

Porridge almost fainted. "Oh, caged inside as well! Oh!"

"Where's the Songsnatcher?" Sally asked the guard. "Why hasn't he killed us?"

"It's none o' your business, but you're not the target."

Target was a pretty neutral word in the Wild North, but not when it meant the kids. Sally had to bite her lip to stop herself biting at the guard instead. Oh, he was lucky there were bars there.

"Let me see my kids!" Mary Bucks begged, her first words in hours.

"You won't be seein' them again," the guard stated. He had no emotion about it, not even callousness and cruelty. It was as if this was a routine operation, a simple job to be done, an order to be followed. The lambs might've been going to the slaughter, but the farmer didn't blink an eye.

The guard left, and Sally's posse sat defeated in their cell, crowded on top of one another. Every one of them there wondered what the children felt, alone in a cell like that, or squashed together like they were. They didn't know why they were there, and they didn't know what was going to happen to them.

"Oh, I can't live like this," Porridge said. He got up and stepped over the others, which wasn't easy to do with the space available, and even less so with the shoes he was wearing. He paced back and forth, climbing over everyone in his way. "I don't do four walls on the best of days, blueberry bunch, but this is agony! Oh!"

They didn't disagree, but there wasn't a lot they could do. They didn't leave Sally with any more dynamite to bulldoze her way out. They were starting to think they might instead have to hear the far-off voices of their children as they brought to whatever end the Songsnatcher had planned for them. And the farmer wouldn't be moved by their final bleats.

"Yoo-hoo," Porridge called. He waved his scarf through the bars, grabbing the attention of another of the guards. "What's a strappin' young man like you, pumpkin, doing by caging an old dandy like me? Oh! I'm innocent! Whatever crime it is, that is."

"Shut it," the guard said.

"I would, but you've shut it for me," Porridge said, as he tried to shake the bars. Then he reached through and pawed down the guard's chest, and then at the keychain on the guard's belt. "Oh, it's so big and heavy! Oh!"

It was then that Sally grabbed Porridge and pulled him back suddenly, which pulled the guard too. The guard's head smacked against the bars, knocking him out cold.

"I could've done that," Porridge said.

"But you didn't," Sally replied.

"I was working up to it, cupcake. Oh! Will no one give me *time*?" He posed dramatically at the bars, while Sally reached through to grab the keys.

"They say to strike while the iron's hot," Thomas Hicks said.

"They do, plum, don't they?" Porridge gestured to himself. "But some say I'm the iron. Oh!"

"Got it," Sally said, as she pulled the keychain inside.

Porridge clapped excitedly. "Oh, I knew we could count on you, Sally."

Sally smiled at him. "And I knew we could count on you."

Chapter Forty-six

THE FIGHT FOR THE FLUTE

Sally's posse crept out of their cell and took out a few other patrolling guards. Most, it seemed, were stationed elsewhere, likely protecting the children. Of course, for that, *protecting* was perhaps too generous a word.

They took what weapons they could from the guards and found their way down to the next level. The Songsnatcher had clearly dug very deep in his aim to hide his crimes. But don't you worry that pretty little head of yours. They'd dig deep for him too.

They heard the Songsnatcher talking to his accomplices in the next chamber. His voice echoed down the corridor.

"We don't have much time," he said. "If those lot found us, it won't be long before the Coilhunter finds us too. Accelerate the … liquidation."

The Songsnatcher didn't specify who or what was to be liquidated, but it didn't take much of an imagination to know what he meant. Sally had to stop him, even if it meant she'd be liquidated in the process. At the very least, she had to slow him until the Coilhunter got there. *If* he got there.

"When we go in there," she whispered to the

others, "we need to take 'im by surprise. We can't let 'im play that music again. I don't think he'll just lock us up next time."

"I'll cover my ears, plum, dashing though they are," Porridge said, before wrapping his scarf around his head like a turban. It probably wouldn't have offered a lot of protection, but it was better than nothing. Besides, Porridge prided himself on good quality fabric in his clothes, so that turban of his was thick, drowning out most sound.

The others tried to do something similar, but mostly fell short. A few contented themselves with shoving their fingers in their ears. Pity they needed them to fight. Not that the Songsnatcher would complain.

Sally went in first, keeping low. She hid behind a pile of crates. Laura followed her, and Porridge and the Bucks Family found their way to another pile across the room. The others with them found their own safe vantage points.

"We lost too many men outside," a guard told the Songsnatcher. "We can't keep up with the numbers. The children fight. We sometimes need two or three men to hold 'em down."

"Then shoot them."

"I thought you wanted the demons to go out in fire."

"We have to adapt. So long as they go out, that's the main thing."

It was then that Sally rushed him, hoping to make him go out first. She charged out from her cover and dived at him, knocking him to the floor. Oh, she could still bulldoze plenty. He struggled with her on the ground as she fumbled for her gun. She got it, but then he swatted it away with one of his unearthed singlesticks, before smashing her across the nose with the other. Her blood dripped all over his armour. He knocked her aside, but before he could get up, she did a little snatching of her own. She grabbed that flute of his from his belt.

"Here!" she shouted before she cast the instrument across the room. She wasn't even sure where she was throwing it. And she wasn't sure where it'd land. It bounced in the centre of the room, and the strike echoed through the instrument, almost making its own song.

That was when all the others charged out. Most went for the guards, or for the Songsnatcher to slow or stop him, but were beaten back as he unleashed his second singlestick. Laura ran to Sally to help her back to her feet. And Porridge and the Bucks Family ran for the flute, sitting out in the open, just begging to be played.

But the Songsnatcher beat back all of his attackers. None of them knew the ways of the *askarochi*. None of them knew the power of the round hand. Oh, but their bodies knew it well now, and knew it in black and blue.

Thomas Bucks took up the flute, but the Songsnatcher took out his gun. He fired, but Sally pounced on him, pushing his hand aside. His aim was off, but the bullet still struck Thomas in the shoulder. He dropped the flute, and Porridge dived for it, heels in the air.

Bullets pinged across the room as everyone emptied their barrels. Bodies fell with the casings, and when the guns clicked empty, everyone changed to hands and feet. Everyone that wasn't already dead, that is.

The Songsnatcher knocked Sally and Laura aside and marched on Porridge, who had clambered up and was charging around the room with a clatter. It didn't take long for the Songsnatcher to reach him.

He put aside his singlesticks and wrestled with Porridge, who was stronger than he looked, and stronger than he feigned. Porridge gripped that instrument as if it was one of his favourite hats. He wasn't ever letting go.

"Oh! Let go, you monster!" he cried as they tussled in place.

Then the Songsnatcher kicked him back, but he still clutched the flute in his hands.

"Hand it over," the Songsnatcher said, "or hand over your life."

"Oh, now, cupcake, most men don't object to me holding their flute."

The Songsnatcher raised his pistol, and that was objection enough. Porridge clenched his eyes to match his fists. Some brave souls said you could pry it out of their cold, dead hands. Well, alrighty then.

And that was when the room went dark.

And that was when you heard the sound of something mechanical.

And that was when you knew the Coilhunter had arrived.

Chapter Forty-seven

BULLDOZER NOX

Nox didn't just enter with a posse. He entered with an army. The mechanical sound didn't just come from one toy duck. It came from a swarm of them as they waddled and rolled into the room. Most were decoys, sure, but the Songsnatcher and his guards would have a lot of fun finding out which ones.

When the lights came back on, Nox stood there behind his toys, with Chance Oakley and Johnny Grin on one side, and Eleanor Pickett and the No-gun Marshals on the other.

"You and your toys," the Songsnatcher said, and his tone was scathing.

"You should see the new ones I brought," Nox rasped.

Porridge backed away, stepping over the toy ducks until he stood with Nox and the others. He still clutched the flute tightly in his hands.

"G'day, drifter," Chance Oakley said, tipping his hat to Porridge.

"Oh, Oakley dear, rugged as ever. Aren't you a sight for *sordid* eyes."

"Good to see ya again, old friend," Oakley replied. "Wish it were in better circumstances, mind."

As they spoke, the Songsnatcher circled the room, and the beady, painted-on eyes of the ducks followed him. Oh, and you knew they were watching.

"Give it up," Nox said. "You and your men are outnumbered now."

"We bested ya," Sally added, as she held her broken nose to stop the bleeding.

"Oh, did you?" the Songsnatcher asked, as he glanced behind at her.

"Your music won't work on us anymore," Thomas Bucks said, clutching his wounded shoulder. There were a lot of brave voices coming from the broken now.

"Go on an' give yourself a second chance," Oakley said. "There's been too much wasted life already."

The Songsnatcher humphed. "But why, Oakley, when I still haven't used all my first?"

"Let's just get 'im," Sally said.

Johnny Grin nodded and smiled. "I like that idea."

"Wait," Nox said. "Put these on." He handed out several newly-crafted earmuffs, which could close and open with a switch, so they could hear when they needed to, and shut off all sound when the Song-snatcher attempted to strike. There wasn't enough for all of them, and they weren't foolproof, and hadn't been tested in battle, but they were better than nothing. The Songsnatcher's music might just make you drowsy instead of sleep.

"We have his flute," Johnny Grin said, patting Porridge on the shoulder.

"For now," the Songsnatcher said, and then he struck.

Chapter Forty-eight

ALL EYES AND EARS

The Songsnatcher charged in, quick as lightning, hopping over the army of ducks and pulling on a pair of blackout goggles as he ran. His guards did the same, even as the ducks spread out towards them, threatening to quack. The Songsnatcher was prepared for the Coilhunter. He'd clearly expected this attack.

Nox fired, and Oakley fired, and anyone else who still had rounds left in their chambers fired. But the bullets pelted off the Songsnatcher's singlesticks, or bounced off his armour, or missed the mark entirely as he danced his way towards them.

Eleanor and the No-gun Marshals leaped in front of the others to take the brunt of the Songsnatcher's attack, and boy did they take it. His attacks were more aggressive than ever, raining down on them with a fury and a flurry. He'd lost his magical instrument, so he gripped those singlesticks all the tighter, bashing their raised forearms, striking their knees, and whacking their heads. Eleanor "No-gun" Pickett got some good kicks in, and Helen "All-arms" Clanton was fast enough with her hands to block what Eleanor missed. June "Four-fist" Fisher got a killer blow into the jaw of the Songsnatcher's mask. It broke her hand, but it clearly rattled that criminal too. He stumbled back a moment, and was on the defensive for the first time in this battle.

The others fought the guards, with bullets if they had them, or with fists and boots of their own. They clustered around Porridge, who ran to and fro with the flute, and guard after guard tried to take him down, and ally after ally got there first. And then two fallen guards grabbed at the tinker's shoes and tugged him to the ground. He yelped as he almost lost the instrument in his fall.

"I've got ya," Sally said, as she kicked those guards back to sleep.

Nox cast butterflies here and eyeblinders there and blasting orbs everywhere else. Guards were toppled by his grappling hooks. Guards were neutralised by his snake-traps. Guards were tripped by the army of ducks that crowded behind their feet at just the right moment. He threw everything he had at them, thinning their number, but more and more streamed up from the lower levels, summoned there by the calls and shouts of the Songsnatcher.

It was those guards, new to the fight, who didn't have blackout goggles like the rest. They were there to guard the children, not fight off this horde of attackers. And it was them the ducks flocked to, as if detecting new feeders with crumbs of bread.

"Get your goggles on!" Nox shouted, but some heard him too late, or didn't hear him at all. You see, those earmuffs could betray you too.

The blasts were even more blinding than ever, set off by several ducks at one. Some folk said it was

Mr. Quacky and Mr. Wacky, but Nox had made it a family. A few more quacks for a lot more eyeballs.

Everyone who didn't have sufficient eye protection, enemy and ally, was floored by the blast. They clawed at their eyes, trying to tear out the burning light. It'd fade in time, but time was another enemy, and it wasn't blind at all.

In that moment of chaos and panic, as the Bucks Family rolled on the floor, as Sally and Laura clutched their eyes, as Johnny Grin rubbed his peepers with his fists, as Oakley stumbled back after using only his arm to shield his face, and as the No-gun Marshals dropped to their knees and pawed at their eye sockets, Nox knew that the battle had turned, and not in the way he'd hoped. The new guards were floored, but only he, with his black goggles, and Porridge, with his polka-dot ones, stood unscathed on the side of good.

The Songsnatcher charged at Porridge, whose shrill cry echoed out to the ears of the blinded. They scrambled on the ground for him, knocking into each other, crawling over each other, desperate to defend him and keep that flute under their control.

"Help me, daisies, help me!" Porridge howled. But the daises couldn't help him just yet. And he'd be pushing up some of his own soon enough.

Nox fired his grapnel at the Songsnatcher as he charged after Porridge, but the criminal saw it coming and swatted the metal claw away. Nox ran after him as it recoiled, swinging the wire like a lasso, but his throw missed the mark, and the Songsnatcher bowled Porridge over with a tumble. They fought for a moment, and it was a furious one. Porridge slapped at the Songsnatcher's arms and mask, and the Songsnatcher bashed at Porridge's bruised and bloodied face with those singlesticks of his.

And then Porridge's cry was ended, and his clenched fist, a little colder and deader now, opened just enough for that flute to roll out, and for the Songsnatcher to snatch it up once more and place it to his lips.

Chapter Forty-nine

SHOWDOWN OF SOUND

The Songsnatcher played his music, and there were few immune to the sound. Nox pulled the shutters down on his earmuffs just in time, but his blinded allies couldn't see the Songsnatcher reclaiming his instrument. They could hear the sound though. Only a handful managed to dull those notes.

As people dozed, or people fell into a lullaby stupor, the Songsnatcher retreated from the arena, leaving his ear-protected guards to mop up the remainders. Some were regaining their sight just now, while others were losing their hearing, or losing themselves to the sound.

Nox chased the Songsnatcher down another level, while the battle still raged above.

And then, when it seemed that he had cornered that villain, the Songsnatcher turned to him and placed that flute of his to his lips once more.

It was a good thing the Coilhunter had some music of his own. And this time Nox didn't just have a guitar. He had a drum.

He unleashed the frame drum like a drumslinger, and bashed the sticks against the rawhide drumhead, like singlesticks of his own. The sound it made was unlike any other, and yet it sounded so familiar, for it was his very own tune, played now to a rhythmic beat.

The Songsnatcher tried to answer, but the music of the Apanajo bowled him over, knocking the flute from his hands. He clambered to his feet, surprised and exhausted.

"Where did you learn that?" he asked the Coil-hunter.

"I learned it from the land," Nox answered, and gave him a refrain.

The Songsnatcher was pushed back once more, but this time he didn't topple. He was ready for it, and could weather the music of the ancients more than most. After all, he could play it too.

"You know what they say 'bout your own medicine," Nox croaked. "Hope you like the taste."

But the Songsnatcher fought on, pressing against the force of the music like a soldier in a storm. It was a gale of notes, a hurricane of sound. Those beats struck your heart as much as they struck the drum. And maybe when they'd stop, then so would that ticker of yours.

"That music," the Songsnatcher roared, shouting over the tumult of the tune, "is not meant for you!"

"It sure is meant for you though," Nox said, as he blasted the song anew, stalling the Songsnatcher as he shielded his face against the unseen wind. It was an anthem of ages, a song of centuries, a ballad for a battle just like this.

But the Songsnatcher pressed on, more deter-mined than ever, until he got close enough to the

Coilhunter to unleash his own drumsticks and use Nox's body as his drum. He knocked aside the instrument, and with a flurry of hands, he bashed at the Coilhunter's own, pushing him back and grinding him down. Yeah, there was a new music now, in the crash and the crunch. This was the Songsnatcher's domain, and he struck with a rhythm that no one could match.

And then the Coilhunter matched it.

To the Songsnatcher's great surprise, Nox blocked the next blow and landed his own before the Songsnatcher could strike again. There was no gun now, and no drum either. There were just hands and fists and arms and sticks. And the Coilhunter knew that art just like him.

They fought, block against strike, strike against block, just like they'd fought before, except this time the Songsnatcher couldn't win. Every move he made, the Coilhunter knew. Every blow he attempted, the Coilhunter shielded.

Again and again they fought, and again and again the Coilhunter pushed him back. The Songsnatcher had spent so much of his energy in the previous battles, that he was growing slower in his attacks and sloppier in his defence. It was only a single well-aimed kick that sent the Coilhunter sprawling, but the Songsnatcher was too exhausted to press his attack.

But where Nox fell was where the Songsnatcher would fall next, for just within reach was that waiting instrument. The Coilhunter took up his drum again and played his fateful tune. The Songsnatcher was tired now and couldn't withstand the gale. He was thrown back, and his sticks were thrown from his hands. He reached for his pistols, but those too were blown from his grip. Finally, he was disarmed. Just a man in a mask now. Just another criminal facing the Coilhunter.

Nox turned to him, guns at the ready, eyeing out the gaps between the Songsnatcher's armour, preparing to make one final coda. There'd be no applause. And there'd be no encore.

"Before you do," the Songsnatcher said. "Let me give you a choice."

He pulled on a rope that opened a curtained section of the room. There, far behind and far above, were two giant glass bell jars, slowly filling with water. And there, in one, with a noose around his neck, was little Noah Walker. And there, in the other, with another rope in place, was Luke.

It seemed like the Songsnatcher would have his encore after all.

Chapter Fifty

A DAMN AWFUL CHOICE

The two boys dangled in place, contained in their bell jars, yet held precariously above a colossal drop that would easily kill them. It seemed that the Songsnatcher didn't trust chance. He had several methods of killing made into those devices at once. First was the water that filled the glass. Second was the rope inside to strangle them. Third was the drop itself, with the glass held by its own rope, which was already burning. It was overkill, sure, but it was kill all the same. And the way it was set up, the way it was rigged, you could only save one of them in time.

"Both are demons," the Songsnatcher said, "so why even save 'em at all? It's me you want, right? But you can't have me and them. And you can't have both of 'em. So, who'll it be, Coilhunter? Me? Your boy Luke? Or that other boy who's nothin' to you? A so-called 'innocent', one of those you claim you're fightin' for."

Nox had no answers for those, and no plan either. The seconds were counting away as he tried to study the mechanisms far up, but they were too far to see. He'd already decided to let the Songsnatcher go—for now. He'd slipped away before, and he'd find him again. Besides, from what he could see, there was nowhere in that dungeon to run away to. Just another, deeper, darker level. Just another step closer to the grave.

And yet the seconds brought those two boys closer to the grave also. As the Songsnatcher slipped away, Nox tried to map a way to get them both down, but he just couldn't see it.

There was no time left to think, and barely time enough to act. He fired his grapnel up towards anything in sight, but the hook fell back down to him with a clang. It wouldn't reach. He clambered up several crates to gain more height and tried again, even as the water reached the chest of Luke and the neck of Noah, even as the rope above frayed and the rope around their necks tightened. The grapnel caught on something, and he didn't even test it for stability. He let the recoil haul him up, where he dangled for a moment, like those two boys dangled over the drop.

"Nox!" he heard Luke cry, though his voice was muffled by the glass. Little Noah in the other container couldn't muffle anything at all, because the water was up to his mouth now. He was barely staying afloat.

Nox was afraid to fire his pistol at Noah's glass, in case it shattered altogether, and the support beneath the boy's feet would fall, and his neck would break in the noose. But if he didn't do something now, that boy would drown. He aimed and held his breath, as if he too was drowning. The bullet pierced the glass, letting some of the water out, giving Noah a few seconds more—giving Nox a few seconds too. Oh, but Death didn't mind loaning you a few of those. He'd take away the hours. The days. The years.

Nox tried to look for something between the two bell jars to fire his other grapnel to, but there was nothing there that he could see. Yet he fired into the nothingness, hoping it'd catch on something, hoping that even God himself would reach down a hand and grab the wire. But remember where God was in the Wild North. He wasn't up there above. He was down there beneath where the boys dangled, down there in the grave.

Yet something caught, and Nox let go of his other grapnel and swung to the new position between the two.

"Nox!" Luke cried again, and his voice bubbled as the water reached his mouth. He placed his hands on the glass, like maybe he wanted to place his hands in the Coilhunter's, and be taken away from that awful place, held like the hand of a father, held like the hand of a son.

"Hold on!" Nox shouted. He didn't mean to shout, but he was shouting as much at the fraying rope, where the embers chipped away at the fibres. He was shouting at the glass in Noah's bell jar, which was starting to crack. He was shouting at the water inside Luke's container, which was starting to smother him. He was shouting at God down below, waiting to catch them both.

Nox could fire that second grapnel, which had just clicked back into place, at either of the hooks at the top of those bell jars, but he couldn't fire at both.

He tried to think if he could cut the rope of one, catch it in time, let it down, and then try to catch the other. It felt like grasping at straws, like snatching at air. Oh, he was the Songsnatcher now, his shouts and their cries forming a final crescendo.

And then the ropes snapped.

Nox gasped, and the sound echoed in his mask. He barely had time to fire that grapnel, and barely had time to aim. He was more reliant than ever on his instincts, on his muscle memory. The hook sailed through the air as both boys screamed and sailed to their doom.

It caught the hook of one of the bell jars, and he felt the sharp, painful tug of his arm muscles as he stopped its descent. The other bell jar plummeted far below, with no hook to catch it, no rope to pull it up, no Coilhunter to stop it smashing on the ground below.

It was a damn awful choice. And it was maybe a little more awful that, for poor little Noah, it wasn't a choice for Nox at all.

Chapter Fifty-one

RECKONIN'

Noah's scream was harrowing. It harried your ears and hounded your soul. If you heard it, you knew for certain that there was a song of passing, a music of death that you never, ever wanted to hear. You heard it with more than just your ears. You heard it with your heart. And you knew that when you tried to go to sleep, you'd heard it again, as if sleep was just a little sample of what was to come.

Nox had tried to catch him, had tried to save him, but he knew it was fruitless. He'd already calculated the chance of saving them both, and it was zero. But it was instinct, not just the muscle memory of the body, but the muscle memory of conscience. You had to try, even when failure was staring you in the eyes. You had to try, because not trying would mean a little bit of you died with him.

Noah perished there that day, and it never should've been. The Songsnatcher escaped again, all because Nox couldn't let both kids die, but there was a larger shadow forming in the back of the Coilhunter's mind: that there were many more Noahs out there, just waiting to be snatched.

Nox lowered the other bell jar to the ground,

released the hook, and swapped for a pistol before blasting that glass apart. The water poured out with the shards, and Luke washed out with them, coughing and spluttering.

And there, across the way from him, in a pool of water and shards and blood, was the broken and bloodied body of poor little Noah Walker, the latest of the Songsnatcher's kills.

When Nox lowered himself to the ground, Luke was already standing. He cradled his arms as he stood over the body of Noah. Maybe he wanted to cry, but no tears came.

"You didn't save 'im," Luke said.

Nox had to clear that lump in his throat. "No."

"You didn't ..." But Luke's voice trailed off.

"I tried," Nox said. "There just … wasn't a way."

"But he was younger though."

"I know."

"You should've saved him."

"I …" Nox sighed deeply. "I saved you."

Nox wanted to embrace him, to comfort him, to comfort himself. But already he felt the chill. There was no victory here. One life saved should've been another point on the good guy's scoreboard, but you should've seen the numbers on the other side.

"What's the point?" Luke asked. "It's just … I ..." He sighed. "What's the point?"

"I don't know what the point is for everyone, but I know what it is for me," Nox said. "It's to make this here land a better place."

"But it's not better, is it?" Luke whimpered.

Nox said nothing. How could he answer that? How could he lie to that?

"Every day it's another murder," Luke said, and he had tears in his eyes. "Every day it's another rape."

A child should have known nothing of murder. A child should have known nothing of rape.

"And you," Luke said. "You're not makin' it better."

Nox bowed his head a little, to hide his eyes, to hide his shame.

"I'm tryin'," he whispered.

"But you can't fight 'em with the law," Luke said. "There is no law."

"There's always law. There has to be."

"But why? What if it's just anarchy? What if we gotta get 'em before they get us?"

"That's the code *they* live by. We need to fight for somethin' better."

"But we're losin' that fight, Nox. We are. And that code o' yours is gettin' people killed. You wait 'til they commit a crime. You wait 'til they get too powerful. All of 'em, they're ... they're a scourge. You can't be gentle with a scourge. We've gotta wipe 'em out."

"We?"

"Well, you're not gonna do it, are ya?"

"What you're speakin' of is genocide."

"So what if it is?"

"It's wrong."

"It's a lesser wrong than what they do. It's a lesser evil."

"But it's still evil. It's still wrong. It's still lawlessness and chaos. It's no better than them."

"Maybe you're right, Nox," Luke said, and he

sounded more resigned than ever. "But there's a lotta kids here like Noah who'll just never know."

WHEN THE MASK FALLS

The Songsnatcher had got away, but he didn't get far. That was the problem with a bunker like that. It was good to hide in, but there was nowhere to run. Nox followed him into his final den. After all that'd happened, oh, he'd make it final, that was for sure.

The Songsnatcher stood there in the gaslight. His armour was chunky and formless, crudely made by unskilled hands. He'd lost his flute, and lost his singlesticks, and lost his guns, and there in that grim lighting, in that grim bunker, he didn't look so strong at all.

"Your time has come," Nox rasped. "And not too soon."

"Don't think I didn't know that it'd end like this."

"Well, that's a surprise. Most criminals think they'll get away with it."

"Well, I'm not most criminals, and if you really understood me, Coilhunter, you'd know I'm not a criminal at all. What I've done, what I've tried to do, is for the good of all. Even you. You don't see it yet, and maybe you never will. But it doesn't matter. I don't need to be remembered."

"Oh, they'll remember you alright, but for all the

wrong reasons."

"It doesn't matter, Coilhunter. I've culled 'em, those demon spawn."

"Do you really believe that, or was that just an excuse for your crime?"

"Do you really believe they're not, or is that just an excuse for your ignorance?"

Nox shook his head. "I don't get your type."

"Good," the Songsnatcher said. "We're not supposed to be *got*."

"But I did get you in the end."

"Only the body. My soul will rest soundly."

"Don't be too sure of that," Nox rasped. "I ain't lettin' your soul go either."

"So, what are you waitin' for? A confession?"

"I think we'll read that on your blood-covered hands."

"So, what then?" the Songsnatcher asked. "You could've killed me by now. I'm disarmed, and you've got new weapons. You want an explanation, huh? Somethin' to make it all alright? Or maybe you want to know who it is behind the mask?"

"Do you not ever remove it?" Nox asked.

"Do you not remove yours?"

"Well, a man's gotta eat."

"What makes you think I'm a man?"

It was then that the Songsnatcher removed his mask. Except he wasn't a *he* at all. It was a woman there beneath that cover. She shook her long, auburn hair out as if to prove the point.

"So, one more surprise, huh?" Nox asked.

"No," she said. "It just shows how little you

understood me."

"Then make me understand, before I make you your final bed."

"I was a mother once," she said. "Or I would've been, if it weren't for the Harvest. When the Iron Empire came, I lost my baby, like thousands of others. Some called it the Great Miscarriage, but I call it the Great Murder. See, you don't believe they took over our birth channels, but I *felt* it. And you're just another man who doesn't know how it feels. And you'll never know. And you'll never feel it. And you'll never know that loss."

"I know that loss," Nox said, and his voice quivered a little. He thought of little Ambrose and little Aaron, and their little fires snuffed out in a greater fire. And he thought of little Luke, who'd almost joined them.

"It's not the same, Coilhunter. You felt that loss from outside yourself. I felt it from *within*. But to make it worse, not long after I signed up to the Resistance, I was captured by the Regime and imprisoned in the Hold. For *fifteen* years. She should've been fifteen too. I should've gotten to hold her and raise her, and see her become a young woman, and maybe see her have a child of her own. But that was all taken from me, and replaced with *them*. It was only when the Iron Empire fell, only when the Resistance finally freed me, that I was able to get my revenge."

"But you didn't, did ya?" Nox said. "You were robbed of a child, so you robbed others of theirs. That ain't revenge. That's a crime. You're just as bad as the Iron Empire."

"Don't say that!" the Songsnatcher cried. "Don't

ever compare me to them!"

"But you just continued their work. They're gone now, and yet you're still killin' our young like you said they did."

"It's not the same," she hissed. "*They're. Not. Ours.*"

"Well, we're never gonna agree on that. You can't ever make me think my kids were demons, just 'cause they were born after the Harvest. You can't ever make me think they weren't mine. I lost them, but I won't lose the good memories of them."

"Then you're a fool, Coilhunter. You think you're fightin' on the right side, but you're not. You're helpin' them. Some day they'll be back. Some day they'll take over again. And you won't even realise it'll be the children you set free who do it."

Nox sighed and shook his head. "You're mad, ya know."

"This whole world is mad. I'm one of the few sane enough to see it."

"You're part o' the reason this world is mad."

The Songsnatcher scoffed. "And you don't think you are?"

Nox would've smiled a little with his eyes if it weren't for everything he'd seen so far, everything he'd tried to stop the Songsnatcher from doing, all those crimes she had to pay for.

"The music," Nox said. "How'd you find it?"

"My family were Apanajo, on my father's side. They might be gone now, but their legacy lives on. I was taught the power of music from a young age. And when I was freed from the Hold, I travelled the

Cactus Wastes until I found the old settlements my father once spoke of. It was there I found the flute."

"One more question," Nox said. "How'd you learn that *askarochi*?"

"One of the No-gun Marshals of the time, Dakota King, was locked up with me. She lost her child too, but at least she had her art to keep her goin' in there. She taught it to me, as a fellow descendent of a tribe, and we practised it for years, before she perished of hunger. It was only vengeance that kept me goin'."

"I know that feelin'," Nox said, "and I know how it can rob you of everything you've got left."

"I don't have anything left," she said. "I'm like the desert. I'm all outta tears. I'm all dried up."

"You could've had more to give."

"I gave what I could. I did what I had to. It was my only way to honour my daughter."

"Well, I'm sorry for your loss," Nox said, "but I ain't sorry for this."

He held his pistol up towards her head and clicked the trigger. Oh, he knew that music well. It was the last note they all heard. He alone heard the echoes.

Chapter Fifty-three

THE ECHOES OF THE ANTHEM

The Songsnatcher was dead, but her legacy would live forever. She hadn't just snatched children from their cradles. She'd snatched lives away from the young. You couldn't get those back. You couldn't trade her body for the countless bodies of those she'd killed. All you could do was be thankful that you got there quick enough to stop her killing more.

Nox returned to the others, who'd mopped up the remaining guards. Sally was there with a bandaged nose, and Porridge was there with blackened eyes, but both were still alive and kicking. Well, maybe they'd had enough kicking for now. Oakley was playing mother, tidying up all their wounds. And there were a lot of wounds to tidy.

They scoured every floor of that prison. They found dozens of cages with children crammed inside. They found dozens of baskets filled with bodies too, and a crematorium set up to dispose of more. It wasn't clear how many had already been burned there. They would just join the list of the "missing," which was a long list in the Wild North—and getting longer by the day.

The Bucks Family found their twins, little Joyce

and Jamie, and they hugged like they'd never hugged before—as if maybe they'd never hug again.

Sally and Laura hugged Luke, and he didn't brush off their embrace. He was shaken by the experience, it was clear, but just as clearly he was glad to see them. They avoided the topic of little Noah altogether. There wasn't anything you could say.

Other families were reunited, and other children were taken home by the No-gun Marshals, or by Nox, Oakley, and Porridge. And in some towns there were celebrations long into the night. And in some homes there were the low-key celebrations of another family meal, of another bedtime story, of another tucking in their kids to sleep.

And in some homes there was no celebration. As they heard the cheers and party music playing next door, they instead stared at the empty beds of their own children, or out windows at the empty landscape, still hoping against hope that one day they'd come home.

But just remember where you were. This was the Wild North, after all.

Chapter Fifty-four

FOR OLD TIMES' SAKE

Back in the Burg, Harvey the Hound hosted a dinner for the Dust Barons, who gathered by the dozen around his table, with him at the head. He wasn't quite one of them, but that didn't mean he couldn't play pretend.

The Dust Barons laughed and talked over each other. They ate and drank more than their fill, while others starved in the streets below. One of them, Baron Flint Fingers, played with coils on the table as if they were toys.

"More ale!" Harvey the Hound told Grapevine Bill, who floated around the room and topped up everyone's drinks. Bill didn't have any of his own. Serving Harvey was liquor enough for him.

"More meat!" Harvey ordered, and Grapevine Bill brought out another large, overflowing platter of cooked chicken, turkey, ham, and duck.

"More fish!" Harvey commanded, and Grapevine Bill brought out another similar platter of salmon, cod, and trout. The room stank up with the smell, but the Dust Barons had gotten quite used to that. To them, it was the smell of wealth.

Then the oil lamps flickered and went out.

"Hey Bill! Tend to the lights there, will ya?" Harvey barked.

But Grapevine Bill didn't tend to the lights. His tall, thin silhouette was exchanged for another, very familiar outline—that one with the cowboy hat, the oxygen tank, and the steel-plated guitar.

"What game is this?" Baron Ed Deadeye asked, as something like the barrel of a gun pressed against the back of his head. His one good eye stared forward, while his bad one tried to search around in the back of his skull for his attacker.

"I don't like this one bit," Baron Broadbelly Jim added, as another barrel came out of the dark for his head too.

One by one, there was a gun barrel for the heads of each of the twelve Dust Barons. And as for Harvey the Hound, well, there was the Coilhunter's dark, intimidating shape behind him. He didn't even need the gun.

The sound of a wind-up toy filled the room, drowning out the muted whimpers of the Dust Barons. Children loved that mechanical sound, children like the ones the Songsnatcher had taken, children like the ones lost to the Dust Barons' funding.

Something climbed up onto the table. It might've been a toy. It might've been a monster.

The light flickered on and off, controlled by the Coilhunter. He let them see just enough to let their imaginations do the rest. They'd all be children to-night.

It might've been a mechanical monkey holding a basket. It might've been a wind-up human holding heads. It might've been your worst fear come to life.

There was the sound of a dozen items tumbling out onto the table.

"Take one," the Coilhunter rasped.

Those Dust Barons didn't even know what they were taking, but they reached out like men reaching out for life. They fumbled in the dark with each other's hands to pull one of the items towards them. They were familiar, just like the Coilhunter's silhouette.

"Hold 'em up," Nox told them.

They did as he said, and there was just enough light now to tell that they were Sam Silver's demon detector devices. Except these ones had been modified by the Coilhunter. Who knew what they could detect now.

"Use 'em," the Coilhunter ordered, and you knew it was an order, like you knew Death didn't ask questions or give answers.

Some of the Dust Barons pointed the devices at themselves. Some of them pointed them at their fellow comrades. At least two of them pointed up at Harvey the Hound. Not a single man there dared to point at the Coilhunter, afraid at what he'd point back.

One by one, every device flicked back and forth from human to demon, and landed on demon in the end. But the cogs still worked inside, and if you listened closely you'd hear the ticking of parts. Maybe some day that ticking would stop. Maybe some day it'd surprise you.

"Let me give you some advice," Nox said, as he placed his gloved hands on Harvey the Hound's shoulders. "For old times' sake."

The Hound couldn't help but shake. If anything, Nox's hands were keeping him steady in his seat. Where he couldn't run. Where he couldn't hide. Where he couldn't fight.

"Don't ever ally with a snatcher again," Nox warned. "I don't care 'bout your reasons. I don't care 'bout your explanations. Don't give me a reason to come back here. Don't make me explain it with lead."

As Nox left the kennel of Harvey the Hound, climbing down the side of the building like a cat, there was someone else watching him with eagle eyes and the barrel-eye of a gun. Cactus Candy took aim from one of the roofs of the Burg. She had a perfect shot for a perfect kill. But don't think she was the only one with eagle eyes. Before she could hit that trigger, she heard something mechanical behind her, small and down low.

And then she heard it quack.

Chapter Fifty-five

THAT FAMILIAR MELODY

A fter Nox had said his goodbyes to the good and the bad, and sent that drum back to the wise girl who gave it to him, it was time to go back to the Bounty Booth to cash in all those many kills. The Coilhunter's mechanical carrion birds had already delivered a rake of bodies, and he had a few more in the bounty box on his monowheel to add to the pile. The Songsnatcher's body took pride and place there.

"Talk about a mountain," Johnny Grin said, as he strolled outside to greet him. Nox wasn't surprised to find him there, and wasn't too shocked to find him there first. But that was the thing about him. You couldn't win the race if you ran off the track.

"Guess I built a bigger one," Nox croaked. He gave the slightest tilt of his head to that one body strapped to the back of Johnny Grin's hyper-hog. It wasn't anyone of note.

"You're good for another year yet," Johnny Grin said, and that almost might've been a compliment. "But we'll save you a spot in the pastures just in case."

"That's kinder than most," Nox said. "The criminals usually dig me a grave."

"Well, what can I say. I'm the kind, compassionate

225

type."

"Maybe you are."

"Was that you bein' kind and compassionate to me?"

"Maybe it was."

"Well, how 'bout that? Partners in crime after all."

"Maybe not in crime."

"True enough, Coilhunter," Johnny said with a laugh. "So, what's all the hype about that song o' yours?"

"What hype?"

"Well, it sends shivers down the spines of anyone who's heard it, or so folk say."

"Let me guess," Nox said. "Ya wanna shiver?"

"Wouldn't mind knowin' it, before you're too old to play your axe."

So, with those lightning-fast reflexes of his, the Coilhunter pulled round his steel-plated guitar and rested his fingers on the strings.

And you should know that tune by now. It started with a twang, like the click of a trigger. It followed with a rhythm, like the ride across the desert. And it ended with an echo, like the voices of the dead. Yeah, if you were a convict in the Wild North, you knew that tune all too well. And after the Coilhunter claimed his latest coils and rode off once more into the sunset, and you sat back and watched him until he became that silhouette they all feared, and you put down your drink, and you closed that book of yours, you might've thought you heard it too.

THE END

ABOUT THE AUTHOR

Dean F. Wilson was born in Dublin, Ireland in 1987. He started writing at age 11, and has since become a *USA Today* and *Wall Street Journal* Bestselling Author.

He is the author of the *Children of Telm* epic fantasy trilogy, the *Great Iron War* steampunk series, the *Coilhunter Chronicles* science-fiction western series, the *Hibernian Hollows* urban fantasy series, and the *Infinite Stars* space opera series.

Dean previously worked as a journalist, primarily in the field of technology. He has written for *TechEye*, *Thinq*, *V3*, *VR-Zone*, *ITProPortal*, *TechRadar Pro*, and *The Inquirer*.

www.deanfwilson.com